The Bigger Picture

Augustus Cileone

Cover Art © 2018 Sage Words Services Copyright:
http://www.123rf.com/profile_zoomzoom'>zoomzoom / 123RF Stock Photo<a
https://www.123rf.com/profile_kohanova'>kohanova / 123RF Stock Photo</a>

Edited by Jake George

A Sage Words Publishing Book
www.sagewordspublishing.com

ISBN-13: 978-0997096286
ISBN-10: 0997096284

Dedication

To my caring wife, Cheryl, a strong and resilient woman.

Prologue

April 1, Noon

Vince Singleton valued his privacy. But now his life was anything but private. He enjoyed taking unnoticed walks to the local Starbucks and ordering his favorite drink, white chocolate mocha. He could only tolerate decaf or else his heart would pound like a Ringo Starr drum solo. He was grateful that he could still get in a stroll on a weekday afternoon with only a few of the neighbors assaulting him with questions. He told himself it would surely get better after the commotion surrounding his recent book died down.

He admitted to himself that he was proud of the novel he wrote several years back. *The Different Drummer* received some critical attention and a small following of outsiders who identified with its social alienation theme. Turns out in the modern world of social media, even a publication with meager sales can attract a deadly fan. The killer left clues relating to movies at the crime scenes. Vince never thought that his lifelong fascination with films would help him solve a murder mystery. Which led to the release earlier in the year of Vince's nonfiction work, *Out of the Picture*. A book about an actual serial killer can really make your profile high. The publisher wanted to ride the wave of curiosity. And that was why Vince was pressured to have this interview with Roman Huston. The thirtysomething journalist was now sitting in the family room of Vince's house in the usually peaceful

Montgomery County suburb of Whitemarsh just outside Philadelphia, Pennsylvania. Huston wrote for *The New York Times*, and it was hard to say no to *The New York Times*.

After sipping some coffee, Huston turned on his tiny digital recorder and began with some easy background questions. Vince knew that the soft balls were just to throw him off guard for when the hard ones came at his head. Having his brother Jake as a reporter made him familiar with the tools of the newspaper trade. Yes, he grew up in Philadelphia and had a good relationship with both his parents who were now deceased. No, he did not initially want to be an English major. He wanted to either be a doctor or a lawyer, but he became attracted to literature because it seemed to reflect all aspects of a culture. Besides, he always liked reading stories. Vince provided the obligatory list of favorite novels, including older works such as *The Great Gatsby* and *Brave New World*, and more recent ones, like *A Handmaid's Tale*. He said his job as a public school English teacher was not always rewarding, because the students seemed to lack motivation. So, when he retired he took a part-time instructor job at Philadelphia Sacred Covenant University.

"And that job was offered to you by your old college friend, Stanford Patterson, the Provost," said Huston. "What persuaded you to take the position, since you were disappointed by students in the past?"

"I was hoping college kids were a bit more mature, having had to excel to get into higher education," said Vince. "Also, nothing initiates young people into modern American culture better than the need to apply themselves while incurring a mountain of debt."

"I had heard that you had a sarcastic edge," said a smiling Huston.

"Some people have been on the cutting side of that edge," said Vince, returning the smile.

"Didn't you and Patterson share a love of movies, and wasn't the film festival he initiated at the college part of the reason you wanted to teach at PSCU?"

"There was that, too," said Vince.

Huston then asked questions about Vince's love of motion pictures dating back to when his father took him many times to the movie theaters, and how he incorporated his film knowledge into classes, exploring adaptations of literature to the screen.

"And Patterson was the first murder victim of your student, Cassandra Kimble, and the deaths of two other faculty members followed. Can you comment on why Cassandra was drawn to you and committed her acts of violence basically for your benefit?"

Here come the fast balls, thought Vince. He tried to step out of the batter's box.

"I'm not a psychologist. It's hard to say why people behave the way they do," he said, knowing that his pathetic stalling couldn't last long.

"But sources say that you have met with Ms. Kimble in prison, and have helped her with her own writing. Why have you supported the young woman who tried to take your life? And aren't you glorifying a murderer by telling her story in your book?"

Vince's first impulse was to end the interview and retreat into his domestic sanctuary. But he knew he had to defend himself.

"I am not glorifying her actions. I want them to be understood. She experienced years of sexual violence which warped her views toward all men and convinced her of the need to punish males who rejected her and harmed other women."

Huston decided to throw a changeup.

"Speaking of mental issues, how is your post-traumatic stress disorder doing? Are you still haunted by witnessing the accidental shooting death of your wife by a policeman?"

"That's 'alleged' accidental shooting. As you know, I have been suspicious of the circumstances surrounding the supposed mugging that took place. I believe it may very well have been a setup because my wife, Jewel, who worked as a psychologist for the police, may have had incriminating evidence regarding some police officers."

"And that information was privileged, and patient records are missing, so you have no actual proof. Is the policeman who worked on the Cassandra case, Lt. Raymond Newman, who has become your friend, trying to unearth the seven-year-old case surrounding the death of your wife?"

"Yes, he is," said Vince.

"Everything going okay with your daughter and Gina Alimentare?" asked Huston.

"Things are fine with my daughter and my girlfriend," said Vince, not wanting to elaborate on his current personal life. "And to answer your earlier question about my psychological health, it's quite good right now. It's amazing how much your life can improve when there are no longer murders occurring around you."

Chapter One

July, Wednesday Night

The predator followed Kate Lawrence to her townhouse just off Rittenhouse Square after her usual long workday as a senior partner at her Philadelphia Society Hill law firm. *She earned that position by assuming sexual ones*, thought the attacker. The approach was quiet. Wearing hiking sneakers was the right choice. They made no scraping noise against the pavement. Practicing how to move without causing clothes to rustle paid off. The attorney was putting her keys into the lock of her door as the dark-clothed figure injected the animal tranquilizer into her carotid artery. Nice penetration, with no spillage. Neatness was important. How well her shapely, fortyish form fit into her dark blue and gray business suit, and she was wearing one of her signature silk scarves around her neck. How professional she looked on the outside, but to the person who saw beneath the fashionable exterior, she was part of the oldest profession. Her long dark hair was slightly damp due to the summer heat. The assailant recognized, from prior stalking, the woody musk scent of the Aerin Iris Meadow perfume the lawyer used, but the pleasant odor could not cover up the stench of her true nature, which would soon be extinguished.

The drug incapacitated Lawrence, and she melted into her captor's arms. The pirated software made bypassing the house's security system easy. Despite the task at hand, the intruder could not help but marvel at the swirling design in the marble oval floor of the entryway atrium. It complimented the dark cherry wood trim and crown molding encircling the area where pale yellow walls met the white ceiling. Nothing modern could ever outdo traditional design. Too bad poor Kate would not play by the tried and trusted rules of female behavior.

The place was spotless and tidy. The smell of ammonia, which might assault some, made the place smell freshly sterile to the assailant. But, it was a sham, wasn't it? The promiscuous woman's life was anything but immaculate, becoming pregnant at age sixteen, and abandoning her baby son, giving him to strangers. How could she throw her child away, like a piece of trash? And, her sleazy ways continued as an adult. There were those late-night liaisons with males dining at Morton's and Ruth's Chris, and then sleeping with them later at The Ritz-Carlton. How slutty. Maybe worse of all was representing that serial killer, that female abomination, Cassandra Kimble.

The intruder grabbed Lawrence under her arms. The lawyer's 120 pounds of weight made it easy to carry her up the staircase to the large master bedroom. Maybe the ornate oriental furniture there would impress others, but the killer would not allow its seductive beauty to be a distraction. After placing the woman on the four-poster king-sized bed, her underwear had to be removed and her outfit replaced with a white dress. To tie her arms behind her with her personalized scarves it was necessary to acquire an additional one from the bedroom closet. In death, Kate must look the part she was destined to play.

While whistling "Stand by Your Man," the killer placed other items, which were stored in the backpack, around the bedroom. The murderer put on vinyl pants and a raincoat, along with latex gloves and a plastic shielded hazmat helmet which was retrieved from the backpack. One must have the appropriate costume to play the role properly. The killer pulled out the weapon, an ice pick, straddled the unconscious Kate, and stabbed her with deep plunges into the throat and chest. The scarlet liquid gushed, soaking the bed covers and splattering the bed board. The murderer's blood drenched apparel was placed in a trash bag which would be incinerated later that night.

Now, there was the exit through the back door and down the alleyway, and a blending into the welcoming dark night. While leaving, the killer thought about how Kate Lawrence must have felt safe and secure in her lovely home. Just like a movie, it was an illusion.

Chapter Two

Early Thursday evening

He loved looking at her. *Well, what's not to like?* Lt. Raymond Newman thought to himself. Samantha Hoffman had thick, shiny blond hair and intense blue-gray eyes that could nail a guy to a wall. Newman was no mountain climber, but he loved scaling her long sculpted legs, majestic breasts, and high cheekbones. On top of that, she was a brilliant college professor. *Why did I put that part second?* he questioned himself. The answer was easy. *Because I'm a guy. But does that excuse it?* He blamed his second-guessing on reading Vince Singleton's blog about sexist attitudes toward women.

He especially liked that she loved to eat. Anything. She was ravenous. Just like him. She caught him looking at her with a smile as she sucked in the last strands of spaghetti in her plate, vampire style.

"What?" she asked, the blood-red tomato sauce staining the sides of her full lips.

"Nothing. Nothing at all," said Newman.

"Hey, you finished before me. I'm glad that doesn't happen in the bedroom," she said, with a quick eyebrow raise. "And, if I wanted to clock your pasta consumption I would need a stopwatch."

She wiped her mouth and paused before speaking again.

"So, you think we'll come out of this date alive, tempting fate? Eating at Reggio's? I mean it's a little

14

bit morbid dining next to the place where Vince's wife was killed?"

"Hasn't hurt your appetite," he said with a grin.

"Nothing can kill that. After almost two years of dating, you should know that by now."

"I'm surprised you didn't comment earlier about the location,"

"I didn't want to say anything because you haven't wanted to talk about it. All I know is that Vince suspected the policemen involved in the shooting of his wife were part of some kind of conspiracy, and it took place close to here."

"I picked the restaurant because it's close to your townhouse," Newman said.

"Yeah, sure, that's the reason. I think the evidence shows that this cold case is overheating your brain."

"Sounds like you've been reading that forensics book for writers," said Newman, referring to the gift he had bought her. "You still interested in writing that CSI type of mystery novel? Like I said, your biology background will really help you there."

"I guess I should let you change the subject, but I think it's better to have you vent. Why don't you tell me what's going on with your investigation?"

The waitress arrived and asked about dessert. Samantha declined but was surprised that Newman didn't order any. They asked for cappuccinos, the lieutenant making his a decaf.

"There was some really tasty looking rum cake on the cart. I'm surprised you passed."

"I still have almost a case of those donuts you bought me. Good thing I have a large freezer," Newman said.

"Thought you would have finished them by now. It's been, what, a couple of days you've had them?"

"Very funny. You know it's closer to a month. I will probably have one before I go to sleep tonight."

Newman hesitated before he resumed talking about work. He ran his hand over his hawkish face and through the close-cropped brown hair.

"I've been feeling guilty about shortchanging our relationship with all the extra hours I've been working, all of them unofficially. Which means I only have myself to blame. I guess I didn't want to cut into the time we do spend together with shop talk," he said.

"Like you said, we're in a relationship. I want to be involved."

Newman thought for several seconds.

"It might help to have some feedback other than what I get from my dad," he said.

"Well, I know I'm not going to be as helpful as an ex-cop, but I'll give it a shot," Samantha said.

"I know that target practice has made you good with a gun, but hold your fire," he said.

They both laughed before Newman spoke again.

"It's been a slow process. I have other cases to work, so it's been difficult finding the time to check out Vince's suspicions. He does make some interesting points. Why did the two alleged thieves have knives instead of guns when they tried to rob Vince and his wife? Why did one of the men hit Vince, knocking him away from Jewel when the couple offered no resistance? The policemen just happened to show up at that time, but didn't use their weapons until Jewel was alone in the line of fire as the crooks fled."

"I know you talked to the cops. Anything come out of that?" asked Samantha.

"Nada. One of the officers, Ned Edmunds, said they were just on patrol. His partner, Patrick Campbell, was the one doing the driving, and had stopped near here because he said there were some muggings in the area."

"Was that true?"

"Good question. I think you should write that book," he said. "There had been a couple, because the alleyway next to this restaurant is a secluded spot. But, there hadn't been any criminal activity in months."

"What did Campbell have to say about that?" she said.

"First I had to track him down," said Newman. "He left the force, but didn't tell anyone officially what his plans were after leaving. I asked around and found out he started working for the "You're Safe" company, an outfit that provides security for places that handle money, like banks, casinos, racetracks, etc. He had been suspended at the time of Jewel's death, since he was the one who did the shooting, but was cleared. He was none too cooperative when I met him. Said he didn't have to say anything to me, which is true. But my gut tells me he's hiding something."

They sipped their cappuccinos.

"What about the two crooks?" Samantha asked.

"Gone guys," said Newman. "Vince couldn't give much of a description, it being a cold winter night, and the men wearing bulky coat hoods down over their heads. He just said the men were big, Caucasian, and both had matching dark beards. Which makes me think they were disguised. No witnesses."

"So, what do you do now?"

"Work hunches," he said. "If Campbell is the one who is dirty, he would have had to work out a deal with the thieves. Maybe he had something on them and used the leverage to get help on the ambush. Luckily, since my captain has cleared things with Internal Affairs, I can work the case on my own. So, I'm looking at arrests

Campbell made in recent years prior to the shooting, and any persons interviewed shortly after Jewel's death."

The waitress brought the bill. It was her turn to pick up the tab, so Samantha placed her Visa card on the small tray.

"I can see why this case is time consuming, going through all those records," she said.

"That's only half of it," said Newman. "The department sometimes hires private psychologists to counsel police officers. Therapy sessions are mandatory following incidents where police officers used deadly force. Jewel was one of those therapists. What is suspicious is that computer files dealing with her PHPD patients were stolen not too long before her death."

"Where does that leave you?"

"Luckily, the billing records weren't taken. Vince gave me those, and I collated the names on those files with police officers, past and present. I have also looked up department records to see what cops were referred to Jewel for compulsory counseling. Coincidences anyone? Turns out Campbell was one of them. He was assigned to her following a shooting. I've been talking to some cops who met with Jewel and may have a connection with Campbell. It's possible Campbell thought what they could have said to Jewel he interpreted as a threat."

"I bet you're a popular fellow around the precinct," Samantha said with a chuckle.

"Yeah, I was already treated like I had the plague when I became chummy with Vince during the Cassandra case. Things eased up after we took her down. But, now that I'm resurrecting his cop conspiracy theory, the cold shoulders are back."

Samantha reached across the table and grabbed his hands.

"Maybe you need some warm arms to be wrapped around you," she said, finishing her statement with an open mouth and a quick flick of her tongue.

"You're killing me here," Newman said. "You know right now I'm using the evenings to catch up on paperwork and I need to get enough sleep on the weekdays, or I'm no good the next day."

"As you said I live close by," Samantha pressed.

"Which makes it easy for me to take you home," he said.

Chapter Three

Thursday, early and late evening

The woman wore a lacy, black negligee. She stood in front of the open window, its curtains flapping in the breeze, like the wings of a bird. The handsome, blonde man entered the dimly lit hotel room. He appeared confused. She asked him if he would be the best there ever would be in the game. He said yes, as he had told her on the train. The woman pulled some of the lace draped over her head down in front of her face, looking like a hooker in mourning. She then pulled out the gun which she was holding behind her back and shot the man in the upper left part of his chest, near the shoulder. He collapsed onto the floor in slow motion. A look at the window showed that the woman was no longer in front of it.

The shot of the window froze. The image on the screen went white. The lights came on. The people sitting in the room facing the projection area squinted, trying to get used to the bright illumination. Vince Singleton walked to the front of the class. He pushed a button on a remote in his right hand. The screen ascended, revealing the writing on the blackboard behind it. It read, "I am a magician. I make cell phones disappear."

"I know, when that bright light blasts your eyes it feels as if you've broken a pupil, or two," he said with a smile. "There ought to be a dimmer in here so I can ease you all back to the harshness of reality. But the first thing to focus on is the message on the board. Cell phones are too distracting for car drivers, walkers, and, most of all, movie theater patrons."

He paused before continuing, using a handkerchief to wipe the salty perspiration which had dripped from his upper lip into his mouth.

"Also, I want to apologize for the stuffy atmosphere in here. The thermostat seems to be broken. I did inform the office about getting it fixed. Since this is summer, I have just shown a scene from a film about the boys of summer. You were all told to watch *The Natural* before attending this class. Would you say our shooter here, Harriet Bird, played by Barbara Hershey, is, as we would say in literature, a well-rounded character?"

Hope waived her somewhat sweaty hand in the air so hard that Vince thought she would get windburn.

"I'm not going to call on my own daughter just yet, since that would be, well, nepotism."

"It's not like we're applying for a job here," called out Hope.

"How about we let someone I have not sired answer the first question."

Vince looked over the grey and white room with its stadium style seating that facilitated viewing the raised platform lecture area facing the rows of seats. There were thirty-five students, several using the laminate flip-over desktops to take notes on their laptops (which could not access the internet – Vince had made sure there would be no Wi-Fi service). The class filled up soon after it was open for enrollment. The registrar's office of the Main Line Movie Academy informed him that five hundred people had applied for the non-credit course. The popularity of the course was due to his encounters with serial killer Cassandra Kimble. But he had to take responsibility for the added attention since he collaborated on the *In Cold Blood* style book which he co-wrote. At least he could share the blame with his journalist brother, Jake, and his film studies professor friend, Vernon Solomon, who helped with the project. It was interesting that it was Jake, the non-movie fan, who had come up with the title of the work – *Out of the Picture*. Now Vince and Vernon were working on the screenplay, which would only contribute to this newfound notoriety.

Stop bullshitting yourself, Vince thought. *You wouldn't write if you didn't want people to read.*

He walked closer to the other students to see the name tags of those who had raised their hands. There was a thirtysomething brunette named Jennifer Walsh. A balding middle-aged man, named Jeffrey Shestack, smiled at Vince as their gazes met. The redhead who appeared to be in her twenties with the name of Debra Pearl waved her arm vigorously. One tag, attached to a broad-shouldered young man of average height with somewhat large ears seated in the front row, stood out because it contained a first name, middle initial, and last name: Ike M. Lacy.

"Mr. Lacy," said Vince, "I haven't heard of an 'Ike' since President Eisenhower. What's your answer to the question?"

"Well, I'm no authority on this topic, or any topic, really, but I would say no, Harriet is not a fully developed character," said Lacy. "Maybe, she's sort of allegorical, or mythical."

"I don't know about other topics, but you show insight on this one, Mr. Lacy," said Vince. "Right you are. The whole film is presented in an other-worldly, mythical way. Robert Redford's Roy Hobbs is a hero with super powers, wielding a baseball bat that reminds one of King Arthur's sword, Excalibur. So, what archetypal role does Harriet play?"

Vince noticed a young nerdy looking African American young man with large eyeglasses shooting glances at an attractive class member with short blonde hair and gray-blue eyes. Her name tag displayed "Pauline Josephs." Vince approached the fellow and discerned his name. Although he understood the appeal of the young lady, Vince called on the young man, hoping to redirect his attention.

"What about you, Mr. Bill Herrman. How about focusing on the question," said Vince.

"She's most definitely a femme fatale," said Herrman. "And it's appropriate that her last name is 'Bird,' since, you know, she flew out of the window."

"Yes, she's a femme fatale – the fatal woman," said Vince. "A female who lures men into dangerous situations. Later in *The Natural,* Hobbs says to the temptress, Memo Paris, played by Kim Bassinger, that they had met before, meaning she was just like Harriet. Both characters drain the man of his heroic powers because they do not want him to achieve his goal of being "the best there ever was" in professional baseball. Homer's Sirens would be primal examples of this archetype. But, so is Eve in the Bible, seducing Adam away from God's laws by urging Adam to give into his appetites and bite that apple full of "carnal knowledge," the title of a film we don't have time to discuss. And so, we come to the theme of this class: How has Hollywood portrayed women who do not conform to established sexual roles? Let's have Dr. Solomon elaborate on this topic."

Vince moved aside to let his fellow instructor, and co-author, Vernon, step in front of the lectern. He was counting on the infusion of recent writing fame to transfuse public speaking confidence into his self-esteem deprived colleague. Vince had to admit that Vernon did look relaxed in his casual blue pullover shirt and khaki pants. His oversized plastic frame eyeglasses did make him appear more of an egghead than did Vince. And, even though they were both in their fifties, Vernon gave the impression of a man several years older than Vince. Vernon's hair had gone gray faster than that of President Barack Obama's. *I guess losing your wife to a fellow worker, getting fired, and becoming suicidal can age a person,* thought Vince to himself. But, with his wife's new man gone (courtesy of Cassandra), and Vernon's literary star starting to shine, he and his ex-wife were becoming, if not romantic, at least chummier.

Just as Vernon was about to speak, the door to the classroom was pushed open, and Vince recognized a familiar face approaching. The middle-aged woman with salon-styled blonde-white hair wearing clothes most likely bought at Neiman-Marcus walked up to the platform with a piece of paper and handed it to Vince. Even though she did not resemble Mary Tyler Moore's Beth from the film *Ordinary People*, Vince felt they both had as much emotion as a mannequin. She did not offer a smile or an apology for interrupting the proceedings. Somehow, she appeared quite cool, as if immune to the feverish heat in the room.

Vince looked at Hope, who mouthed, "What's she doing here?"

Vince also wondered why Faye Patterson, the widow of the former Provost of Philadelphia Sacred Covenant University, and Vince's friend, Stanford Patterson, wanted to take this course. Even though he had helped to capture Cassandra, who was Stanford's ex-lover and killer, Faye had been vocal about not being one of Vince's fans. He looked at the enrollment form handed to him.

"Hello, Faye," said Vince. "I was told that this class was closed."

Faye aimed her battleship-gray eyes at Vince.

"Since I have now taken over Stanford's position as the coordinator of the PSCU Film Festival, I was given a special dispensation to attend. I could use some brushing up on my movie knowledge," she said.

Vince didn't know that Faye, unlike her husband, had any film background to bring into the foreground. He smiled.

"Well then, why don't you try to make yourself comfortable and take a seat," he said.

The Provost's widow walked up a couple of levels and found a spot in the middle of the seating area. The row she chose seemed to mirror her chronological stage in life, and Vince thought his descending desire to scale theater steps also dated him. He heard Lacy say in a distinct voice to the girl next to him, "We don't need any more bodies in here. They better cool down the heat real soon, or it's going to feel like Florida in July in this place."

Ike saw that Vince heard his remarks. He leaned forward in his seat and said in a lower voice, "Maybe you could get a filled ice bucket in here, Mr. Singleton, so we can chill our water bottles. If I overheat, my clothes develop sweat stains. I hate that."

"Think cool thoughts," said Vince. He then stepped up to the podium and spoke into the microphone.

"Again, Dr. Solomon," he said.

Vernon walked to the podium and adjusted the mike, which produced a feedback whine. He pressed the remote to lower the screen and accessed the PowerPoint display with controls on the podium. A still showing Humphrey Bogart and Mary Astor appeared on the screen.

"Ah, I'm sure most, if not all, here have seen *The Maltese Falcon*," said Vernon. "Mary Astor's character fits into the, um, femme fatale category, mentioned earlier. She appears dependent, fragile, but it is all a ploy to lure men into helping her reach her criminal goal of acquiring the titular 'black bird.' She, well, sexually seduces Bogart's Sam Spade. She does not play the stereotypical married, husband-supporting, monogamous female that society rewarded when the movie was made. So, in the end, she must 'take the fall,' and go to jail."

Vince mused that Vernon still couldn't get rid of those James Stewart speech hesitations, despite his many years in the lecture hall. Well, Vince didn't like standing in front of people, either. Maybe that was why he zipped through his book signing public appearances – he wanted to escape as soon as possible.

Vernon pressed the display button, and the Medusa-haired Glenn Close, holding a knife, replaced the previous slide.

"*Fatal Attraction*'s Alex (notice the, um, male name – telling you she is not being what was once considered appropriately feminine), is the cautionary nightmare the male of the species will encounter if he strays into the extra-marital, ah, passion trap of the aggressive man-eater. She, too, is punished at the end of the film. Justice is carried out by the faithful, socially accepted role-playing character of the wronged wife. By the way, people, do you know where your pet rabbits are?"

There was laughter. *Good, he's using humor,* thought Vince.

The attractive Pauline Josephs raised her hand, at first flitting her nail-polished fingers, but then, rolling them into a fist, and punching the air.

"Yes," said Vernon.

"Don't you think that men have forced women into using their assigned feminine roles to get what they wanted from the male-dominated world?" she asked.

"A good point," said Vernon. "It was in the movie, ah, *Dolores Claiborne* that the title character says women are given the role of, ah, excuse the term, 'bitch,' by men, so sometimes that is all they have left to get anything they want done. In that film, Kathy Bates' Claiborne carries out her revenge against her husband who is one of the worst kind of female abusers, an incestuous predator. We will be exploring this theme of the sexual roles imposed on women, and their attempts at emancipation from such roles. Specifically, the class will see a progression of change in the depictions of sensual women, from being presented as villains, who had to be punished, to portrayals of liberated, physically passionate females, who were also wrongdoers, but who escaped prosecution for their anti-social acts, to characters who were decent people who simply sought carnal gratification on an equal level as their male counterparts."

Vernon then summarized some of the other movies that would be examined, which included *Mildred Pierce, Looking for Mr. Goodbar, Klute, Thelma and Louise* and *Working Girl*. He took several questions from the class and then handed the mike over to Vince.

"Thanks, Dr. Solomon. In addition to those touched on, we will also be analyzing motion pictures, such as *Basic Instinct* – easy men – *Body Heat, The Last Seduction, The Accused, The Piano*, and others, which explore the depiction of women in terms of their sexuality in Hollywood films. Those intelligent people who have read my blog posts will already have flipped on the switch to enlightenment on our topic. See you next week."

As the class began to empty, Hope came up to Vince.

"Not a bad start, Dad," she said. "I'll give you pointers on how to improve your delivery when I get home."

"There's nothing to point to," he said with a smile. "I'm glad you are still talking about coming 'home,' even though you're apartment hunting."

"Well, it's time for your house to become my home away from home," she said. "How did it feel being in front of a class again?"

Even though Vince had many years of teaching experience in the public schools and continued part-time at PSCU after his retirement, he felt out of place, like Robert De Niro coming home in *The Deer Hunter*, being an instructor again. He liked to blame his recent teaching sabbatical on his writing, but the fact was that he was shook up after the Cassandra business. It had already been tough enough dealing with his wife's violent death. The loss of Jewel left a void that was tough to fill. *Sometimes I don't think I'll ever be me again. I'm not even sure who that person is*, Vince said to himself.

"Yeah, well, it is a little strange. It helps that it's a non-credit course. At least I'm not messing with anybody's GPA," he said. "Thanks for attending and providing moral support."

Hope said, "Always there for you. Except for now. I'm going out for some pizza with Mark, James, and Evan."

"Say 'hi' to the movie geek gang for me," said Vince, as Hope waived as she left. "Text me if you get home before me."

"Have a nice evening with Gina," called Hope as she approached the exit.

Vince felt a warm wave of affection wash through his body any time her name was mentioned. Gina Alimentare and he had come a long way from bantering back and forth in the office they shared at PSCU when Vince was teaching there part-time. He didn't think he could ever feel love for another woman after what happened to Jewel. But, he was starting to feel as if he had been wrong. Hope had given him a ride to the class and Gina was picking him up in a couple of minutes. They were going for a late meal at The Eat-In–Take-Out Diner in Bryn Mawr. Vince loved having breakfast food any time of the day, and he had the urge for the brioche French toast with blueberries and whip cream on their menu.

Vince told Vernon before he left that he would meet him in two days to work on the screenplay on the weekend. Vince approached Faye Patterson as she was ready to leave and told her he was glad that she was attending his class.

"I'm here for the class, not you, Vince," she said without even looking at him. "I do not understand how you could aid the person who killed your friend. Helping Cassandra Kimble with her writing, publishing blog posts urging the death penalty not be carried out. And, your association with that Hoffman woman is a personal affront to me. That academic slut who threw herself at my late husband should be fired for her lack of morals. You should be ashamed of yourself for your connections to these dirty stains on the purity of decent women everywhere!"

Faye strode out of the classroom. She was not alone in her frustration with Vince's attitude toward Cassandra. Gina, Hope, and others, online and in person, were critical, too. Lt. Raymond Newman wondered why the man whose help he had accepted to catch the female serial killer now wanted to aid the person who also tried to off Vince. As for biology professor Samantha Hoffman, she was, as her current beau Newman would agree, a smart woman who was as sexual as any man, and who defied the double standard between the sexes that seemed to refuse to die. However, she did fall in love with the married Provost, Vince's friend, whose philandering ways Vince did not discover until after his death. He could understand Faye's anger, but not her dismissal of her husband's complicity in his infidelities.

He hoped that he could eventually make his girlfriend understand why he saw something in Cassandra worth redeeming. Before he became bogged down in doubts, Vince went outside. Gina was already waiting for him in her green Ford Focus. Before he could make it over to her car, a tall, lean young man approached him. He was one of the class members. Wide open eyes matched the young man's broad grin. The name tag said "Joe Goldman." Familiarity tapped at the backdoor of Vince's brain, seeking entrance.

"What a thrill it is to be in your class, Mr. Singleton," he said in a rush. He grabbed Vince's hand and started shaking it up and down so fast, Vince felt like a water pump. "It's going to be the bomb."

"The bomb? Well, let's hope your mind doesn't explode from absorbing too much wisdom," said Vince, detaching himself from the youth's circulatory depriving grasp.

"My name is Joe Goldman," He looked down at the tag. "Well, obviously, you can read. I've commented on many posts on your film blog. I met you before at one of your book signings. It was at the Barnes and Noble in Conshohocken. I'm whooped up about the movies we will be discussing."

Now Vince remembered. This guy placed a crazy number of responses to film discussions on his site. He recalled they were mostly about mysteries or thrillers.

"Yes, I thought you and your name looked familiar. Well, I hope we can meet your 'whoop' expectations," Vince said. "I have to catch my ride there."

He pointed to the Focus.

"Great meeting you, sir," said Goldman. "Can't wait for the next session."

He then ran off.

Vince walked over to Gina's car. They exchanged smiles and they kissed after Vince settled into the passenger seat.

"Looks like an enthusiastic student. What was it like teaching again?" she asked.

"Not bad. I felt a little shaky. I'm primarily a literature guy after all, not a film studies professor. Vernon was a big help, and I was grateful that Hope was there," he said.

"Aw, look at you being all vulnerable," said Gina.

"Only around you," he said in a low voice. After a short pause, he said, "But, you're not going to believe this – Faye Patterson is in the class,"

"Get outta here," said Gina, giving him a Julia Louis-Dreyfus-from-*Seinfeld* shove.

"Easy there, Elaine," he said.

"Did the dingo eat her baby?" said Gina.

"You really get into the character, don't you," said Vince. "And, the dingo line originally comes from the

Meryl Streep movie, *A Cry in the Dark.* Another film about a misunderstood woman."

"Yeah, Yeah, of course it does, Mr. Movie-Know-It-All," she said. "And here's the DVD you wanted. It was on sale at Target, like you said."

Gina handed him a copy of *Hanna*, the 2011 action film.

"So why did you want this movie?"

"I love stories that have females kicking butt. Even if the female in this case is a teenage one who is genetically engineered. Usually they kick male behinds, but in this one, she also finishes off Cate Blanchett. But, Cate acts like a guy in this flick, so it works for me."

"Hm, maybe I should sign up for a martial arts class," said Gina.

"I already know you can take me, but I am aroused. Thanks for picking up the movie," Vince said. "And how was your day?"

"About time you asked," she said. "The students in July classes are sleepier than I am. The real snoozing comes later when I have to read their essays."

"Come on, you love doing your comparative lit thing," said Vince.

"I miss my office roommate," she said, giving Vince's arm a squeeze.

"Hopefully I'll be back soon," he said, returning the affectionate grasp. "Hey I'm hungry. Point me at that French Toast."

"Yeah, with a side of bacon!" said Gina as she put the car in gear.

The food was delicious, dripping with syrup and calories. The restaurant, like most diners, was open until late, so they talked for quite a while about literature, and, of course, movies. Vince felt his cell phone vibrate in his pants pocket.

"It must be Hope," he said as he pulled the phone out and looked at the screen. There was a text, but it was from an unknown person. He read it, and stopped breathing for several seconds. He looked around the dining room, his senses kicking into heightened alertness. Sweat started to flow down his forehead. Gina saw the change in him and was alarmed.

"Vince, what's wrong?"

He read her the message.

"Contact Lt. Newman about the woman's body that will be found later tonight. You will follow the clues. And, your collaboration with the police must be public. They're going to write books about it. If you don't participate, just remember, you can't protect your women."

Chapter Four

Thursday Night

After a failed attempt at being current with his case files, Newman changed into his blue pajama pants and Philadelphia Eagles T-shirt. He sank into his black leather sofa in his Fox Chase apartment and watched some of a Phillies baseball game. He already defrosted and ate one of the powdered sugar covered jelly donuts that Samantha had bought him, each enclosed in a wrapper that said, "For Cops Only." He had drifted off when he heard his cell phone ringing. A bit annoyed, Newman looked at the ID. Vince. He was going to have some fun with him.

"What the hell, man, it's kind of late. You're making me lose sleep, and I love my sleep."

Newman was surprised Vince ignored the reference to the Laurence Fishburne line in *Mission Impossible III.*

"Ray, I just received a disturbing text."

"You must be upset to not note a movie quote," said Newman. "What gives?"

Vince told him about the text. Newman considered what he heard for a few seconds.

"Don't dummy up on me, Ray," said Vince, and Newman could hear panic in his voice. "I'm scared for Hope and Gina. I'm here with Gina right now at a diner. I contacted Hope. She's with her friends at Mark Goodner's apartment. I want them protected."

"Calm down, Vince," said Newman. "You received weird messages before from crazy people since Cassandra's arrest and after the release of your book. This is probably just another crank caller."

"The line 'you can't protect your women' is from the movie *The Jackal*. It's delivered by Bruce Willis' character. He plays a professional assassin, Ray," said Vince.

Newman let out a loud sigh. That feeling of dread that he had when things went sideways started to creep through his insides.

"Okay, okay. I'll contact headquarters and ask if anybody has received a call about a dead person tonight, especially a female one. Tell Hope to go home, and have Gina stay at your place tonight. I'll have a car sent over there. I'll be in touch."

After hanging up, Newman started to call the office. So much for getting a good night's sleep.

Chapter Five

Later Thursday Night

Detective Ben Smartley of the Philadelphia Homicide Division felt he should have been a lieutenant by now. Hell, he *knew* he should have been. He could get things done. He had done a damn good job as a soldier in Iraq. And, he was doing a hell of a job as a detective. Solved a lot of cases. He could sniff out the story behind the clues like a mental bloodhound. But, his annual evaluations always came up with that same old crock of shit – that he didn't "mesh" well with other cops, wasn't a good team player. What the hell was this – little league baseball? Nothing was ever good enough for the guys behind the desks. His ex-wives and former girlfriends used to bellyache about him not being a people person. You could never satisfy them, too, the bitches.

Instead the higher-ups promoted that adolescent Newman. That young punk acted like he always knew it all. So he helped solve that Kimble case. Big deal. He had just been lucky. And now Newman was breathing down other policemen's necks, investigating the death of that pain-in-the-ass Singleton's wife. Internal Affairs was letting him get away with it, too. It had all been settled years ago. Smartley had made sure of it. Well, Newman was getting too close. When the anonymous phone tip came in about that left-wing, ACLU-Planned Parenthood-loving lawyer, Lawrence, Smartley started to think that pulling the late shift this night showed that luck might now be on his side.

Smartley knew Newman and Kate Lawrence were involved a while back. And she was the one who ended it. Info about her hookups circulated through the office gossip go-around. She was a real mantrap, that one. Admittedly, Smartley had felt pleasure at hearing the news that Mr. Wonder Boy had been dumped. Although the two had been involved, Newman and Lawrence weren't making music together all the time. It sounded more like angry noise when Newman testified in court against a few of her clients. Smartley had to say that the couple of times he saw them in court, she didn't pull any verbal punches when she cross-examined her boyfriend. Newman definitely would make a plausible suspect as the killer. Smartley knew the man's habits. The guy was doing double duty, working his own cases and looking into the Singleton shooting. He took work home and stayed in late at night playing catch-up. Good chance he would not have an alibi.

He hustled himself over to the captain's office and talked the old man into assigning him the case. He also knew he had to work fast to carry out his plan. He looked around Newman's desk for something useful, but found nothing. Then he saw something in the trash can. It was a personalized donut wrapper from Newman's current gal. *That'll do it*, he thought to himself.

Smartley had his own prepaid phone to cover his ass. He scrolled for Patrick Campbell's number, and placed the call.

"This better be somebody I know who has this number, or I'm going to be mighty pissed."

Smartley chuckled.

"Hold onto your urine, Campy. It's Ben," he said.

"Can this wait? I'm working late here doing the security at the Chester County Casino."

"Even though I'm glad to hear that an ex-cop can still make a living, the answer is no, this can't wait. It's about Newman," said Smartley.

"Bastard!" said Campbell. "You don't think he'll get to us, do you?"

"No, I got a way to get to him," said Smartley. "Now that you're in that cushy job, do you still remember how to work a frame?"

"To save our hides? Absolutely," said Campbell.

"Meet me at Walker's Deli for breakfast tomorrow at 8 am."

"Your treat," said Campbell.

There was a loud click on the other end of the line. *Cheapskate*, said Smartley to himself.

Chapter Six

Before Dawn, Friday Morning

Lt. Raymond Newman had drifted off to sleep on his couch when his cell phone started playing the theme song from *Rocky*. His hand shot out like a fighter's jab to answer the call, but he had no desire to eat raw eggs and run up the Philadelphia Art Museum steps.

"Yeah, you got something?" he heard his raspy voice ask.

"You ain't gonna believe this one." It was his dad's old friend at the station, Sergeant Jim Fisher. Newman would believe anything the senior cop had to say.

"Okay, give it to me." Newman could feel his stomach muscles tightening.

"It's your old flame, Kate Lawrence."

Newman removed the receiver from his right ear and reflexively stuck a finger in it, as if trying to unclog it. He must have misunderstood Fisher.

"What? Who did you say it was?"

"It's Kate Lawrence, Ray. I'm really sorry."

He flashed to her long dark hair flowing in the wind in her Corvette. He saw her smiling with a cup of cappuccino in St. Mark's Square in the photo she had given him. Then his mind resurrected that buried thought of the night she called it off. When had he talked to her last? Six months ago? It was at City Hall, about a case. It was okay between them, had been for a couple of years. And things were great with Samantha now. Still, he felt a sinking, almost panicky feeling about this death. He shook it off. He was then able to see the connection to Vince.

"Ray, you there?"

"Where did it happen?" he asked, his voice clearing up.

"At her place. You know, near Rittenhouse Square."

"I know."

Newman thought for a minute.

"Who's heading it up?"

"It's Harvey Douglas. High profile case, so he's taking lead on it."

Douglas was pretty much a by-the-book guy. Fair, from what Newman knew of him. Still, you never could tell.

"Anybody else?"

"Yeaaah." Newman could hear the bad news in Fisher's dragged out monosyllable. "Ben Smartley got his stocky butt in gear and was in the captain's office quicker than a rhino in the jungle."

"Damn," said Newman. "I have to be there."

"You can't. You were involved with the victim."

"I've got important info. Thanks for your help."

"Think about this, Ray, You can't …"

But Newman hung up before he could hear any more.

***

Detective Smartley arrived early at Lawrence's house. Harvey Douglas was already there, talking with the guys from the Forensic Sciences Division in the living room. He slipped on a pair of light blue latex gloves. Smartley went into the empty kitchen and planted Newman's donut wrapper in the wastebasket.

He then walked upstairs and looked around Kate Lawrence's bedroom. Smartley walked closer to the bed. The dead woman was on her back. *Given that she slept around, it wasn't an unfamiliar position*, he thought to himself as he gave out a dismissive snort. Part of the pale-yellow sheets looked like they were washed in red. Underneath all the blood that had poured out of her body, Lawrence had on a flowing white dress. He could see some of Lawrence's pulled back dark hair peeking out under a blond wig. There was a set of underwear next to the body. Someone had stretched pajamas out on the bed next to the victim. *Did the killer do this to say he had put her permanently to sleep*? thought Smartley. There was a book next to her head. Smartley bent down to get a better look. The title was *Dangerous Seductions.* From the title and the picture of the half-naked couple on the cover, Smartley guessed it was some sort of an erotic novel. He wasn't surprised she was into some porn. But, he had to consider that the murderer planted the book. The killer tied her hands behind her with Lawrence's own scarves, each monogrammed with an italic "*KL.*" *And why, for Christ's sake, is it so hot in here*? Smartley asked himself.

Someone must have read his mind because he heard one of the men there say, "Hey, Esterhaus, crank up the AC, will ya'? You would think being a hotshot lawyer she wouldn't have to scrimp on her electric bill."

Smartley realized it would be difficult under any circumstances to pin a murder rap on a police lieutenant. He had hoped the Lawrence woman's death would look more like an act of passion. But, this was planned out with cold calculation. Not likely a policeman would be sloppy enough to leave incriminating evidence at the site. But, he also knew that cops had to follow the evidence. The process of analyzing everything in the townhouse for prints, DNA, etc., had already begun. He knew his little addition to the investigation would soon be found. Smartley searched for a few bits of incrimination to be found at Newman's apartment. One of those monogrammed scarves would work out just fine. He looked through some dresser drawers but didn't find what he wanted. He entered one of the walk-in closets in the bedroom. There was a mirrored compartment along the wall. He opened the door and found wine red, pastel blue, and forest green silk scarves displayed in a drawer. They all contained the "*KL.*" There was one that was still in a tiny shopping bag. He grabbed the scarf and the receipt. *$500 for this little piece of cloth? Christ*, he thought. The date printed on the paper showed that she bought it within the last month. When Newman would say he hadn't seen Lawrence in a long time, the evidence would show him to be a liar. He folded up the scarf, put it back in the little bag, and stuffed it into his pocket, making sure none of the cops was close enough to notice.

He then went to the bathroom adjacent to the master bedroom. It was huge, with a roomy glass shower stall with a gold border around the door, and a rain showerhead. The sunken marble tub was fitted with Jacuzzi jets. It looked a lot nicer than his own claw-footed monstrosity. There were no knobs on the wide beveled glass recessed medicine cabinet. He pressed the edge of the glass and it popped open on one side. He did the same with the other. Inside were rows of cosmetics. He looked at a few lipstick containers and chose one which was already open for the DNA evidence needed to set Newman up.

He heard someone enter the bedroom. He took a look and saw Douglas accompanied by Dr. Terry Stowe from the Medical Examiner's office.

"There is no evidence of a struggle. No defensive wounds," said Stowe. "She was probably unconscious when she was attacked. Not sure yet if she was knocked out or drugged."

"In other words, you don't have squat for me right now is what you're saying," said Douglas.

Stowe ignored the remark.

"With the temperature being very warm in here for so long, it skews determining the loss of body heat. But, I'd say death was around one in the morning. Lawrence was not wearing any underwear, but the initial examination does not indicate that she was sexually assaulted. I'll have more information later after the autopsy."

Smartley could tell that this ME did not like to be rushed.

"Um-hm," said Douglas, "it's always later with you guys. What about the wounds?"

"They were the cause of death. She had a massive loss of blood. By the size of the piercings, I'd say that the killer used a pointed instrument, causing deep puncture wounds."

"Oh my God!" The words came in a deep, shaky voice out of the mouth of Lt. Raymond Newman, who was standing in the bedroom doorway. Smartley rushed over to where Douglas stood, placing his broad back in front of Newman,

"He shouldn't be here, sir," Smartley told Douglas. "Newman was involved with the victim romantically. He should not be allowed to participate in the investigation."

"Shut up." The anger in Newman's voice assaulted the detective's ears. "I have pertinent information to share with Lt. Douglas about this case."

Smartley turned around and faced Newman, baring his teeth before speaking.

"You should leave. Now."

"Smartley," Douglas said. "We need statements from any witnesses who may have heard or seen anything suspicious, tonight or otherwise. Go and check out the neighbors. And can somebody rustle me up some black coffee?"

Smartley made his exit in slow motion just as Douglas spoke to Newman.

"Okay, Lieutenant. Speak."

Chapter Seven

8:30 AM Friday Morning

Smartley was pissed. Campbell was late, as usual. *He probably would miss Judgment Day*, he thought with a shake of his head. But, he would always cut his ex-cop friend a lot of slack since Iraq. Campbell was able to save several guys when he suspected that terrorist bitch near the restaurant where they were eating in Baghdad before he and the other soldiers knew what was going down. She was a clever suicide bomber, pretending she was pregnant, hiding an IED under that bulge. A good example of motherhood, that one. Too bad someone hadn't aborted her life before she could deliver that bomb.

Since then, Smartley felt uncomfortable in restaurants, especially today, sitting with the lipstick and scarf belonging to the Lawrence woman in a bag next to him. He was eyeing the joint, never sure where danger could be hiding, like a submarine ready to fire its payload. But, it was a familiar location, and he knew he should be fine here. Besides, Walker's Deli in the hilly Roxborough section of Philly had great coffee, unlike the sludge at the station. The smoky scent of the meat on the grill jump-started his salivary glands. He enjoyed that tasty combination of sweet and salty as he took another bite of the juicy blueberry pancakes covered in thick Vermont maple syrup, followed by another strip of the crispy bacon. He was taking a gulp of the rich coffee when Campbell's towering form appeared at the entrance. Campbell had a perpetual five o'clock shadow. His mussed, wavy hair had a just-got-out-of-bed look. He saw Smartley, walked over to his booth, and sat down with a thud.

"Lose your watch, Campy?"

"If you recall I didn't stick around for retirement, so I didn't get the timepiece."

"No great loss. All they give you is a piece of tinny crap to wear around your wrist. But, you're doing okay, so buy yourself a Bulova. And invest in a razor and a comb, will ya'?"

"If I wanted to be insulted, I would have stayed married. What gives?"

Smartley lifted his coffee mug, took another sip while looking around the deli, and leaned forward before talking in a low voice.

"Here," he said as he passed the brown bag under the table to Campbell. "Keep the receipt with the lawyer's scarf. We want it to look like she'd seen Newman recently. Put them someplace so they're found, but not too obvious."

"I know what to do. I'm no rookie." Campbell paused and then added, "Anything else?"

"Yeah. I found out the probable doer sent a text to Singleton, telling him a dead woman was going to be found last night. It said that he should contact Newman about it."

"Is that going to be a problem?"

"Well, it puts another wrinkle in the straitjacket. But, once Newman becomes a suspect in the investigation, I could spin it by saying he sent the text himself to throw off the scent."

Campbell shrugged and said, "Spin away."

"I know we can't build a tight case against Newman. No witnesses seeing him with Lawrence lately, and not enough evidence at the Lawrence woman's place. But, if we can make him look shady, who knows? He could at least be a PR problem, and it might get him suspended. Maybe even reassigned with a leash on him."

The waitress came over and offered Campbell coffee. He grunted an acceptance and took a swig as she walked away.

"I know those patient records never surfaced, but I don't like it that they can still be out there for Newman to find," said Smartley, focusing his gaze on Campbell.

Campbell shifted his over-sized body, then met Smartley's look with his own eye slits and a tightened jaw.

"It's not like I didn't look around for them. Linda knew a lot of people, a lot of them guys, the slut. I couldn't put the squeeze on all of them."

Smartley lightly smacked the table with both hands.

"I hope this scheme works."

"If not, we may have to go to Plan B."

Smartley drew back from Campbell's clenched face. He didn't like what he just heard. He shook his head, wondering just how dirty he would have to get before he settled the debt he owed his friend.

Chapter Eight

Early Friday Afternoon

Vince was sitting in the family room of his house in sleepy Whitemarsh Township just outside of Philadelphia. The thought of how he once wanted to live in the center of the large city sprinted through his brain. With the current hyperalertness of his PTSD, the noise there would be intolerable. It's a good thing Jewel convinced him to live among the lawn-insulating properties of suburbia.

He was trying to distract Gina and Hope with stories about improvisations during the making of the Mike Nichols directed movie, *The Graduate.*

"So, when Benjamin is in the sun porch with Mr. Robinson, actor Murray Hamilton hesitates on his next line because he forgets Dustin Hoffman's character's name. Hoffman cues him by saying 'Ben.' Nichols thought it was so funny, probably because it emphasized the lack of communication between characters in the film, that he left the flub in."

The two women smiled a bit, but Vince could see in their eyes the worried preoccupation that had taken up residence in their minds. He tried another story.

"And then there's that scene where Ben is so nervous the first time he gets a room for him and Mrs. Robinson at the hotel. Nichols told scriptwriter Buck Henry, playing the desk clerk, to surprise Hoffman by ringing the porter's bell. Hoffman, startled, reflexively covers the bell after the first ring, and for the second ring, Henry then hits Hoffman's hand instead of the bell."

They again displayed forced grins, which were followed by the sound of the doorbell ringing. Vince thought, *Speaking of a bell, I was just saved by one.* Hope and Gina looked relieved. Even Jellybean, his cat, who usually ran for a place to hide when someone came to the door, woke up from her bored nap and sprang up onto the arm of Vince's chair in anticipation of a change in the situation. Vince had to come up with some better stories to tell. He rose from the black leather lounger and went to the door. He felt relieved to see Newman standing on the other side of the threshold, carrying a bag from Dunkin' Donuts.

"Are those for us?" asked Gina, the other food enthusiast in the group.

"They could be for you," said Newman.

"Ha, he's coming along with the movie references," said an enthusiastic Hope. "That's the line Bill Murray says to Scarlett Johansson in *Lost in Translation.* It's at the hospital when she sees him with the huge stuffed animal."

Newman grinned.

"I brought blueberry and pumpkin muffins. So, you know, there's some nutritious stuff in there somewhere."

"Yeah, buried under all the sugar," said Vince, as he let Newman inside the room. He glanced at the police car stationed in front of the house for protection. *Good. It's still there*, he thought.

"Hey, I bought the low-fat muffins. Besides you need some sugar for energy. Now if we could only figure out how to use it instead of gas in cars ..."

"Then our automobiles would need fuel injection bypasses," said Gina.

49

Vince was grateful for Newman lightening the mood. It had been a tense night after the text he received. He went to the kitchen to Keurig some coffee to have with the treats. After it was brewed, they settled down in front of snack tables with the hot brew and dessert. Jellybean purred and nudged Vince, so he gave her a few pieces of his muffin. Their small-talk about how they were all doing felt forced to Vince, but it helped ease them into the more serious discussion that had to follow. Newman had called Vince as soon as he knew about Kate Lawrence's death. Newman smiled so as not to alarm the rest of them, but, his eyes darted about, as they tried to evade the inquiring faces looking at him. Vince wished this new threat would disappear, but knew things didn't work that way.

"We were going to get some exercise before you showed up, Ray," said Gina. "After those goodies, we really need a walk now. You guys want to join us?"

Newman seemed to always be consuming food, but right now Vince wanted to find out what was eating at Newman.

"You know what, I want to catch up with the lieutenant, here. You two go ahead, and maybe we'll join you later."

"Okay, but I counted the muffins," said Gina. "So, if there are any missing when I get back, you're running laps, Vince."

"Otherwise, Dad, you'll have to hope your body will eat your ass."

"That's my daughter using a line from the Kirsten Dunst cheerleader movie, *Bring It On*," said Vince.

Newman rolled his eyes, and Gina and Hope left the men alone. Vince was all business now.

"So what gives? Did you talk with the lieutenant in charge?"

"Yeah, I did. I don't think I mentioned his name. It's Harvey Douglas. He looks to be a bit of a tight-ass, but I think he's okay. I told him about the text. He saw the connections. Obviously, he knew about you and Cassandra, and knew that Kate Lawrence was Cassandra's attorney."

"Do you think he's going to be cooperative? I mean, from what this killer said in the text, Hope, Gina, and who knows who else could be at risk."

"Douglas isn't just a by-the-book stickler. He narrows it down to doing things by every freaking letter. But, he is taking this threat seriously. That's why, even though you're a civilian, he wants to talk with you about the clues at the crime scene. Bring your cell to see if they can trace the message to anyone. I know they received an anonymous tip about Lawrence, but I'm pretty sure they couldn't track down who called."

Vince sensed a problem.

"What do you mean you're 'pretty sure?' Don't you know what's going on? How come you're not in charge of this case, since it involves me and Cassandra?"

Newman stood up, paced a bit, and rubbed his right hand across his face before he spoke.

"I was romantically involved with Kate Lawrence about three years ago. We met on the job when I was testifying on a case concerning a client of hers. It didn't last long before we broke it off. Well, she cut the cord. She wasn't ready for any long-term attachments. I wasn't either, but didn't realize it at the time. Anyway, because of my past association with her, I am prohibited from participating in the investigation."

"What? Why didn't you mention this before? Why didn't you say that you knew Lawrence when she became Cassandra's lawyer?"

"Hey, I had nothing to do with her representing Cassandra. Unlike you, I'm not in the helping-the-serial killer business. Kate reached out to her on her own; probably saw it as one of her causes. Anyway, Douglas knows I can't be officially attached to the case, but I suspect he assumes I'll be assisting in the background based on my past experiences with you. But, I have to be careful. It can't look like I'm actively involved."

"Sure, I get it." said Vince. "And, thanks. I'm going to need all the help I can get."

Vince paused, knowing any questions might sting, but he wanted to know more about Lawrence.

"What do you know about Ms. Lawrence that might help us understand why she was the victim?"

Newman looked away for a moment before talking.

"Her mother was a lawyer and her father an English professor at Swarthmore College. She became pregnant at age sixteen, but decided to give up her baby son for adoption. I guess she thought she was too young to be a mom. She obviously inherited her parents' scholarly genes. She graduated magna cum laude from the University of Pennsylvania Law School. She did pro bono work for Planned Parenthood, the ACLU, and took on domestic violence cases. She fought against the death penalty. She was briefly married to another lawyer. She never had any more children."

Vince knew he was pushing it, but he asked anyway.

"Anything about her personal life you can add?"

Newman paced some more. Vince was surprised to see a small smile appear on the man's face.

"She loved to eat sushi, especially California rolls, and to drink sake. Her favorite book was *Fear of Flying*, and, although she was not big on musicals, she did like *Chicago*. She would go to Ocean City, New Jersey, each year just to eat at the Chatterbox restaurant with her friends, the same ones who went there with her when she was in high school. But, her favorite place in the world was Venice, Italy."

The smile disappeared from Newman's face.

"She did have a reputation as a player," he said. "You know, romantically."

Vince thought he had dug up enough memories.

"Thanks. Sorry about all of this."

Newman sat down on the sofa and looked relieved not to have to talk about his former girlfriend any more.

"When you find out about those clues, fill me in on them," Newman said. "I have connections at the office, but I don't want to get anybody there in trouble by asking them to spill too much. Do you have any thoughts about why this killer contacted you, or what these clues will be?"

Vince knew that Newman could see the worry on his face.

"It's going to take a while to figure out the plot here. But, I'm pretty sure it has to do with movies."

Newman produced a stifled chuckle before saying, "Here we go again."

Chapter Nine

Late Friday Afternoon

As Vince walked toward Harvey Douglas' office, he tried to keep his eyes straight ahead. But, he still noticed the policemen he passed shot piercing looks at him that could have penetrated body armor. Even though he had helped crack Cassandra's case, he knew many on the force still considered him suspect because of his accusations about officers being involved in Jewel's death.

Vince's first impression of Douglas was that he looked like a younger Tommy Lee Jones, circa *The Fugitive*. After they shook hands, Douglas motioned for Vince to sit down in the chair in front of the Lieutenant's desk. After sitting in his own chair, Douglas spoke, and Vince thought the policeman delivered his words in almost the same rapid monotone with a Southern twang that Jones used.

"I'm going to be up-front with you Singleton. I don't like working with civilians in a collaborative capacity. But, the circumstances here are special. You were texted by someone who is either the killer, or who knew about the death of Kate Lawrence. Since there appears to be a threat ..."

"There was no appearing about it," Vince said. "The line about not being able to protect my women sounds pretty specific to me."

"That is the difference between your amateur subjectivity and a professional law enforcement officer's objectivity," said Douglas. "You told Lt. Newman the quote is from a movie, a movie I have seen. And the primary target in that film was not someone Richard Gere's character previously knew. So, the reference in your text may not be a threat directed specifically at women in your life."

"First off," Vince said, "a female Russian police officer who Gere did become friends with was killed by The Jackal. Second, the texter directed the threat at my world to get me to become involved. Third, there is another ominous reference in the text to another movie, the Clint Eastwood film, *In the Line of Fire*. John Malkovich's assassin tells Eastwood's Secret Service character that they will write books about them after he kills the president. And, fourth, I don't like collaborating with you, either. But it looks like we are stuck with each other."

After a brief pause, Douglas offered a slight smile.

"May I please have your cell phone? I'll get it back to you before you leave. I believe you will be receiving more messages."

"I'm afraid you're right about that," Vice said as he handed over his Android cell.

Douglas took the phone and viewed the text message.

"See, we already agree on something," said Douglas. He went to the door, called a female officer over, said something Vince didn't catch, and handed her the phone. He returned to his chair.

"I'm partial to my iPhone. Due for an upgrade." he said.

"I'm past due. I like to stick with what I know."

"If only the world wasn't constantly filling us up with more knowledge," mused Douglas as his right index finger tapped his cheek. He paused again before speaking.

"First off, I want to ask you what you deduce from the message you received."

"Another audition? I did one for Lt. Newman before. I didn't think I'd have to go through the process again."

Douglas was silent.

"Alright. There is mention made of "women" in the text. Kate Lawrence, obviously, was a woman. And, she represented Cassandra Kimble, another female, who I helped put in jail. So, it appears that women may be targets here. And, I have been drawn into this situation because of my involvement with Cassandra, and, by association, Lawrence. Also, the message refers to a movie quote. I'm a film enthusiast, and helped solve clues pointing to movies in Cassandra's case. How am I doin'?"

"Not bad," said Douglas. "But I think there's more. See, a good policeman must keep on top of things, know what's going on around him. Never know when some piece of information may fit into a larger puzzle of related evidence. I listen to the TV, check out social media sites. And I know that you have been visiting Ms. Kimble, and helping her with her writing. You have petitioned to have her death sentence commuted. You also have posted on blogs about ending domestic abuse of women. And, you are teaching a course about …"

Douglas picked up a piece of paper and read from it.

"How Hollywood portrayed women who do not conform to established gender roles. The description here says that, specifically, the class will 'explore the depiction of women in terms of their sexuality in Hollywood films.'"

Douglas put down the paper.

"How am I doin'?" he said.

Vince arched his brows.

"Not bad."

Douglas pulled out another sheet of paper and handed it to Vince. On it was listed what was found in Kate Lawrence's home: the blond wig; the erotic novel; the white dress; the scarves; the underwear next to the body; the pajamas.

"If you can stomach it, here are some photos of the victim and the objects found near her."

Douglas passed Vince a manila folder. He opened it and flinched when he saw the body and the bedcovers painted in blood. The red color flowed and carried him to that night in the alley. He was there again on that February night, and shivered as he felt the cold take hold of him. His body gave a jolt as he saw Jewel's body being ripped by the bullets. He slammed the folder shut, trying to end the flashback.

"You okay, Singleton?"

Vince at first didn't realize where he was. *Snap out of it Vince*, he said to himself, *focus on the here and now*. After a moment, he returned to the present.

"Yeah, sure," was his almost inaudible response.

"You coming up with anything just looking at what I've given you?"

"Not yet. You've told me what you found. Anything missing? Anything else, say, unusual that you noted?"

"Since we only started processing the evidence early this morning, there will be more information to follow."

Douglas thought for a moment.

"The ME said there did not appear to be a struggle on the part of the victim. We have a working hypothesis that she was drugged."

"Why were her hands bound? No struggle, so no need for restraints."

Douglas again allowed a slight smile to creep over his face.

"I can see why Newman used you before. Good point. Also, the house was quite warm when we arrived there. I was told that the thermostat was set at about 85 degrees. Does that help any?"

Vince just shook his head.

"I know when you worked with Newman he gave you a fair amount of latitude to consult with other people. It worked out well last time. Officially, I can't condone that."

Translated, that meant to Vince that he would use what resources he could gather, but Douglas didn't want to hear about it.

The lieutenant leaned forward.

"You better keep that journalist brother of yours on a short leash. We're not disclosing the discovery of the scarves, underwear and pajamas at the crime scene. No mention of those to the public. You know the drill – we hold back to weed out suspects. Understood?"

Vince clenched his jaw and nodded his head. More sibling dodgeball with Jake.

"I'll let you know if anything new develops. And, you contact me immediately if you get any ... cinematic insights. Also, we'll let it be known that you're involved with the investigation, so the alleged killer knows you are complying with his, or her, instructions. No mention of texts received so you don't start getting copycat messages. Of course, you'll be attracting attention. I guess you're used to that by now."

Vince bowed his head in surrender and said, "No, not really."

Chapter Ten

Saturday Afternoon

The media onslaught had begun soon after Douglas had released the information about Vince's participation in the Kate Lawrence case. His name went viral before and now there was a re-infection. There were phone calls, emails, texts, Facebook posts – all dredging up Jewel's death and Cassandra's case. Vince stonewalled reporters. The police presence at the house kept unwanted visitors at bay.

Of course, Jake called him early in the morning, wanting the inside track on his involvement in the investigation. He told his brother to meet him and Hope at Vernon Solomon's house in West Mt Airy. Gina returned home to change her clothes and was to meet them at Vernon's place. Vince had asked Vernon if he could escape to his writing partner's home for a while, and that he wanted his input on what was happening. He felt that Vernon's knowledge of films would be helpful. He and Hope were driving on Henry Avenue in Roxborough. He was thinking that he was grateful that Hope had just ended her first year as an English teacher in the Plymouth-Whitemarsh school district, where she had been a student. Her being on summer vacation allowed him to keep a safe eye on her.

"I think I better tell you that along with Evan, Mark and James will be at Vernon's place," said Hope.

Vince gave a quick glance at Hope and saw her shrink in the bucket seat of the Honda Civic, as if waiting for a verbal blow to land.

"Why not invite the Mormon Tabernacle Choir, too. We can have a sing-along," said Vince, knowing he sounded irritated.

"Hey, it wasn't my idea. It is Evan's dad's house, and he's hanging out there between semesters, working on his doctorate. And Mark and James are his pals. Besides they all can help with anything having to do with movies."

"How am I going to keep a lid on ..." and just as he was about to finish his thought, a car in the left lane darted across the right lane in which Vince's car was traveling and made a sharp right turn into a side street, just missing slamming into the front of the Civic.

"Idiot," yelled Vince at his windshield. "This last-second exiting is starting to become an epidemic. Why don't these people get into the right lane early on if they know they're going to get off the road. They're probably performing electronic masturbation, stroking their cell phones, oblivious to anything but their mindless texts or another video of a dog dancing with a cat. Technology is a curse."

"Yeah, and you were glad to be Intel-afflicted so you could write on a laptop instead of a legal pad, Mr. Old School." Hope paused and looked at her father. "I know this situation is like way intense. So, maybe it would be a good idea to schedule an appointment with Dr. Probst soon."

He reluctantly began to consider that he may need a few office visits. Since his psychologist had helped in dealing with the loss of Jewel, and the effects of the Cassandra case, maybe he could be of use again.

Hope responded to his silence.

"You got your stealth look on. Have you been getting any flashbacks? Nightmares?"

He didn't like to concede that some of his post-traumatic stress disorder symptoms were starting to reappear. He didn't want to worry Hope, but he always wanted to be honest with her.

"I had a sort of flashback at the police station. I stayed up late last night because I was afraid of having bad dreams. I went into hyperalert mode after you went to sleep, making sure the house was safe. I think I started to get Jellybean paranoid. She was following me around, doing those robot-quick moves with her head, scanning the place, pupils dilated."

"See, you're starting to stress out the cat. We can't have that. Get in touch with Probst."

"Okay, yeah. I'll give his office a call."

"In the meantime, pull into that Starbucks on the right. Some decaf white chocolate mocha has got to help."

At the mention of his favorite drink, he smiled. He pulled into the parking lot.

"It couldn't hurt," he said.

Chapter Eleven

Saturday Afternoon

After the coffee therapy, Vince drove to Vernon's house in Mount Airy. He observed Gina's Ford Focus along with Jake's Prius on the street. He wasn't looking forward to trying to get his reporter brother again to not disclose too much about the investigation. He also noticed James Player's new BMW was in the driveway.

"Nice ride James has there," Vince commented. "Must be sweet to have a dad who is the Superintendent of Philly's schools and a mom who is a famous poet."

"Like you didn't score big time with your book advance and sales, and now the bread you're going to get with the screenplay," said Hope. "Why are you still driving this five-year-old Civic anyway? Go get a Porsche, man."

"First off, the money for the screenplay is not in the bank yet. And second, I'm saving up for an Aston Martin. I believe in investing in Bond's."

"You're more shaken than stirred. You'll probably buy a Volvo."

They rang the doorbell and Vernon let them in. As soon as they entered the living room, Mark Goodner jumped up from the couch, exhibiting his basketball height, and approached Hope, giving her a hug. *She definitely could do worse*, thought Vince to himself, especially since Mark was also an avid film fan.

"So, are we going to talk about the Lawrence case, or what?" asked Jake, disguising his pointed remark with his Dennis Quaid smile. Vince loved his brother, but he envied those movie star good looks.

"I came here to brainstorm," said Vince with a touch of annoyance in his voice. "But, I'm not in the mood for a mental Katrina."

He paused.

"The lieutenant in charge, Harvey Douglas, gave me unofficial approval to use resources to help with the investigation. But, all of you have to keep most of what we say under wraps."

"Jesus, not again," said Jake, shaking his head. "I'm a newsman and holding back on information violates my trust with the public."

Vince admired Jake's passion for worthwhile causes, and Vince shared that enthusiasm, but he felt his brother liked to bolt ahead without considering all sides of a situation. Vince felt the need to reign in Jake, and he knew that made him look like a sell-out to his sibling.

"Don't get me started on how the media violates the public every day with it's slanted, edited, and selective presentation of what it reports to the public," said Vince.

Hope jumped in, performing her usual personality bomb squad role to diffuse tension between the brothers.

"Let's just calm down and stay focused here. Uncle Jake, just let my dad give us what he feels we have to know. He needs our help, as family members, and as friends, first, before we consider professional obligations."

Jake nodded his head, and Vince smiled at Hope. He knew he was so lucky to have her as his daughter. Gina, looking sexy in her tight jeans and snug sleeveless black pullover top, rose from one of the chairs and dittoed Mark's embrace of Hope by putting her arms around Vince and giving him a tight squeeze. He whispered in her ear.

"I'm so glad you're here."

She brushed her lips against his ear and exhaled, "Always."

Hope and Mark sat on pillows on the Oriental rug on the floor while the rest made themselves comfortable on the sofa and matching blue-gray loveseat and chair. Vince looked around the room. The house was clean and tidy compared to the way it was during Vernon's dark time when his wife left him, he was fired, and on a suicide watch. Vince knew that his friend had come a long way since then, with no small help from his son, Evan, who stood by him through it all. Evan and his father brought out juice and soda for everyone and the atmosphere became more relaxed.

"James, I haven't seen you since you landed that film reviewing job with *The Philadelphia Times*," said Vince. "I read a couple of your articles. Not bad."

"Just a part-time gig, don't you know," James said as he ran his hand through his wild black curly hair which looked as if it would never be tamed. Vince observed that the not-so-vertically elevated James couldn't play one-on-one with his fellow film fanatic friend, Mark. "I'm waiting for the big break so I can escape the shadow of the parents' realm of worship. I'm really sick of having to go to those parties they have with everybody fawning over them"

James paused for a moment, his own thoughts interrupting his train of thought.

"Wait a minute," he said. "You only read a couple of the articles? And they were just 'Not bad.'"

"Yeah, I heard you're up for a Pulitzer," said Mark to James, with a laugh. "You better quit while you're ahead."

"Mark, I recently found out that they could use a veterinary student at the animal hospital that Kitty Cove uses. Interested?" asked Vince.

"Sure thing. I have some free time on Monday's. Does that work?"

"Yeah, I'll introduce you to the manager there."

"I think Jellybean is getting jealous of Dad hanging out with other felines," kidded Hope.

"When I come home from volunteering at Kitty Cove, she sniffs me all over and gives me the stinky eye if I don't give her treats to make up for my time at the shelter," said Vince. "I don't want my cat to put me in the doghouse."

After they chuckled at Vince's remarks, Vernon spoke.

"Well, Evan here settled on a topic for his Ph.D. thesis. Tell them, son."

Vince could almost see Evan cringing, as he tugged at the collar of his Izod shirt and ran his hands down the pleats in his khakis. Vince knew the young man was a perfectionist, and probably felt rushed into what he felt was a premature discussion about his work.

"Father, I haven't sufficiently narrowed down the thesis statement yet."

"Well, okay, but, ah, just give them your general topic of exploration, then," said Vernon, his voice sounding like a verbal push.

Evan looked downward and spoke to the rug.

"Okay, it's going to focus on the sexual outsider in films."

As soon as the words trickled out of Evan's mouth, a deluge of suggestions flowed from the other movie maniacs in the room.

"You have to talk about *Maurice*. Merchent-Ivory film from 1987," shouted James. "And, hello, *The Imitation Game* really shows how badly gays were treated in the middle of the twentieth century."

"Like don't forget *Far from Heaven*. Todd Haynes directed it and it has a 1950's take on a gay man. Then he dealt with lesbians in *Carol*," said Hope.

"The lesbian theme is addressed in *Personal Best* with Olympic athletes, and with the gangster gals in The Wachowski's *Bound*," said Mark. "Those chicks were hot in that flick."

Vince saw Hope give Mark a shove which was tempered with a smile. Vince couldn't be left out of the advice avalanche.

"Remember the transgender themes in the tragic *Boys Don't Cry*, *The Danish Girl*, and the not so serious *Transamerica*."

"Please, stop!" yelled Evan. "I know all about these films." And then after a pause, seeking a change of topic he said, "Let's address the more serious business at hand."

Vince nodded and spoke to his brother in a more conciliatory tone.

"Jake, I am sorry about having to keep some details secret, but it's important because Hope, Gina, and maybe others could be at risk."

He then informed them of the contents of the text.

"I understand," said Jake. "And, we'll get through this thing, just like we have in the past."

Vince gave a quick grin and nodded his head in appreciation.

"Newman should be here," said Mark with emphasis. "He was mentioned in the text. Why isn't he running the show? Seems like we have a typical case of police incompetence, here."

"Calm down, Mark," said Hope in a low, soothing voice. Vince knew his daughter usually could calm her sometimes hothead boyfriend. Like Vince, Mark had anger issues dealing with the authorities. In Mark's case, it involved confrontations over demonstrations protesting cruelty to animals.

"There's a wrinkle in the material there," said Vince. "Newman was romantically involved with Lawrence, so he's excluded officially from the investigation. But, it looks like he'll be working with us covertly, and I'll keep him informed of what we come up with, if anything."

Vince then told the group about the clues found at Kate Lawrence's home.

"We're not letting on about the text to me to eliminate getting fake messages from those playful idiots out there who have nothing better to do than to be annoying."

"You're such a people person, dad," said Hope. She added, "And mums the word, or if you prefer other words, like silence is golden, about the scarves, underwear and the pajamas, so the police can filter out phony informants or habitual confessors. Okay, Uncle Jake?"

"Yeah, yeah," agreed the reluctant journalist.

Despite the attempts to keep the conversation light, the dark seriousness of the situation started to permeate the room. There was a period of silence, which Vince decided to break.

"The person who sent the text referred to quotes from movies. Since I was already involved in a murder case where there were clues related to films left at the scenes of the crimes, and, I am currently co-teaching a film class, I think we have to assume that the clues at Kate Lawrence's home refer to movies. So, what motion pictures might they be referring to?"

"There have been a lot of slice and dice slasher films showing women as victims," said James. "Very 'old school.' You really can't have women as victims much nowadays. It comes off as sexist. I personally like films like *The Terminator* or the *Resident Evil* flicks, where gals kick guys' butts."

"Ah, that's interesting, because in our class, we, ah, will be exploring the transformation of women in films from being victims to becoming empowered heroes," said Vernon.

"But don't you think those types of films turn women into men, instead of having them maintain their sexuality?" asked Evan.

"Yes, I mean, that is one of the points we'll be discussing," said Vernon. "As well as --."

"But, don't you think it's necessary to go to the other extreme to counter the stereotype?" said Hope.

"Wait a minute, we're getting off track here," said Vince. "Let's get back to James' point about women as victims. The text threatened women, and a woman was a victim in the murder. Maybe we have someone who wants to return to the 'old school,' as James said."

There was a break in the speculations as Vince felt that each one of them was rifling through movie files stored in his or her brain.

"If there is an attempt to reverse a trend, then maybe the killer is using clues related to a film, but placing a woman as the victim instead of a man," said Mark.

Mark's words opened a cinematic window in Vince's mind.

"That's it!" he said. "The scarves! It's *Basic Instinct.* In that film men are tied up and killed by a woman."

"Yes," said Hope. "Sharon Stone's female predator in that film wore her blonde hair in a way that would jive with the wig placed on Lawrence."

"I'm no movie expert, but even I remember that Stone's character seduced men. And, she killed her lover with an ice pick at the beginning of that movie," said Gina. "We should ask Douglas if that could have been the weapon used on Lawrence."

"And, ah, Stone's character, Catherine Tramell, is an erotic thriller writer, and as, you said, Vince, such a novel was found next to the body," said Vernon.

"And what male could forget the no-underwear scene at the police station," said Jake, with a far-away look on his face that seemed to Vince that his brother was enjoying picturing the revealing image.

Vince thought for a moment before speaking, doubts rubbing against his certainty like mental abrasions.

"What about the pajamas? I don't recall anything about those in the film."

"OMG, Vince is right," said James. "The people in that movie didn't bother with sleep wear."

"Yes, we must be precise about interpreting the clues," said Evan, sitting stiffly upright in his chair. "Vincent, you said the dress was loose and flowing. I believe the garment worn by Ms. Stone was short and form-fitting."

"Yeah, and what's with the sauna temperature in the house?" questioned Hope. "I don't remember the thermostat setting having anything to do with the plot of *Basic Instinct.*"

"Maybe we're not on the right track," said Gina.

There was unsettled quiet in the room, as Jake started to pace, James scratched his tangled hair, and Hope shifted her body for comfort to compensate for the lack of mental relaxation. Vince tried drawing on his limited investigative experience with Cassandra's case. She had left inconsistent film clues at her murder scenes.

"Not on the wrong track, but maybe there are different trains running on several tracks," said Vince. "Remember that Cassandra placed items pointing to the next crime and victim. Since this killer has implicated me in his plans, and made a victim out of Lawrence, who was associated with Cassandra, he, or she, may be repeating that pattern."

"Ah, yes, I see your point, Vince," said Vernon. "But, um, what do the dress, pajamas, and temperature setting refer to?"

Vince shook his head.

"I don't know – yet," he said.

"Well, until you do," said Gina, "I think you better tell Lt. Douglas what you suspect."

"Yes, and update Newman, like you promised," said Hope.

Vince felt his eyes instinctively widen in response to a fear-laden thought that struck him. He reluctantly shared his disturbing perception.

"Not only have I mentioned *Basic Instinct* on my blog, by I also referenced it in my syllabus for the class on Thursday evening."

The others looked at each other in silence. Vince understood that they realized the killer may be close by.

Chapter Twelve

Saturday Evening

Vince saw the police car pull up in front of his house just after he arrived home with Gina and Hope.

"The cops are in sync alright, like Mussolini and his train schedules. I texted Douglas that we would be home around six, and there is the officer at his post."

Gina sat down on the family room sofa, kicked off her sandals, and fanned herself with a copy of *Writer's Digest* before commenting on Vince's remarks.

"I would think you'd feel relieved that he's out there, but you sound annoyed. And, how about turning on that A/C."

Vince moved the thermostat switch to "cool" as Hope walked in with a pitcher of lemonade that she placed on the coffee table. She proceeded to pour each of them a glass of the chilled liquid.

"Yeah, dad. What's with the hostility? You have to keep working on having a positive frame of mind."

Vince took a gulp of the semi-tart cold concoction, but the resultant brain freeze was ineffective in tempering his feverish thoughts.

"I'm grateful for the protection and outraged that we have to have it. And, you know I still don't know who to trust when it comes to the police, after Mom. They're not all like Newman."

Vince's cell phone buzzed, indicating he received a text message. He put in the password to unlock the device and viewed the message.

"Oh shit! It's the killer," he said through gritted teeth.

Gina almost dropped her glass.

"What does it say?" she asked in a shaky voice.

Vince hesitated, then read the text as his hands trembled.

"The police have graciously let it be known that you are onboard with our little project. I am so pleased that you have decided to participate. Though, I suppose I didn't give you much choice. Any progress yet? Oh, and this message is untraceable, like the last one, and those that will follow."

Vince tried to hide his apprehension. He didn't want to spread his fear, but he could see by looking at them that Hope and Gina had already caught it.

"What do you think I should do? Will he/she just get angry if I ignore the message? Try to harm one of you?"

"I think you should say something. Maybe just say you're still working on the clues," said Gina.

"Yeah," said Hope. "If you show, like, you're catching on too quickly to what's going on, it might just cause this person to get more excited, be more violent."

Another buzz, another text. Vince opened it up with dread.

"This one must be reading your minds. It says, 'You will most likely have figured out some of the clues. If you don't share your actual progress, well, as I said before, you can't protect your women.'"

Since the killer gave him no choice, Vince texted the conclusions they reached regarding *Basic Instinct*. The reply was brief:

"Very good. About what I expected. You still have more to discover. Good luck."

After Vince shared the message, Gina walked over to where Vince sat and rubbed his right shoulder. Hope followed Gina and squeezed his left arm. Jellybean also instinctively knew there was tension to be relieved. She jumped onto Vince's lap, rubbed against his face, and purred loudly when he gently scratched her.

"You may not trust most of the police," said Gina, "but, you need help. Call Newman and Douglas."

Vince nodded his agreement.

Chapter Thirteen

Monday Morning

As a former cop, Patrick Campbell learned a great deal about breaking into homes from the thieves he investigated. Smartley told him that Newman would be at the station early, so he waited until after the morning rush hour, when most of the people living at the apartment house would be off to work. For a cop, Newman didn't take too many security precautions. But just as doctors make lousy patients, so do cops fail as civilians. Campbell picked the door handle lock and, soon after, flipped the deadbolt, allowing him to enter Newman's home.

He needed to place the lipstick and scarf so that Lieutenant Wiseass wouldn't notice them, but not so hidden that they looked like obvious plants in a set-up. He glided through the place, trying not to displace anything. He had to admit he liked the Eagles' pennants and logos hung about. He noticed on the wall a frame containing a ticket to one of the 2008 World Series games the Phillies won. *Damn, I couldn't get tickets for that game*, thought Campbell. He was glad he was sticking it to the young punk.

Not that he could ever figure out what goes on in a woman's head, but he guessed Lawrence would stow a silk scarf in a dresser drawer. He went into the bedroom. The place looked too prissy, too uncluttered for a real man. *At least he didn't make his bed before going to work. He may have some testosterone left in him*, thought Campbell. He walked over to the dark wood bureau and started opening a few drawers with his latex-gloved hands. He found a small compartment in the center of the piece of furniture which contained winter gloves. Campbell smiled, realizing that Newman would not be using that drawer in the summertime. He took the little bag with the scarf and receipt out of the small shopping bag he was carrying, placed Lawrence's purchase under a pair of Isotoners and slid the drawer back in place. He then went into the hallway and found the bathroom, but knew some lipstick in a medicine cabinet would be too obvious for Newman not to notice. There was a door on the left-hand side of the vanity cabinet. He swung it open and saw shelves that pulled out. They were full of soaps, aftershave, sunscreen, body creams and unopened toothpaste boxes. He took the lipstick out of the shopping bag, making sure not to smear Lawrence's fingerprints, and placed the tube under the body cream containers. Campbell thought it wasn't likely Newman would need to moisturize his skin in the summer, unless he really was a closet homo.

He headed for the apartment door, and slowly opened it. He peeked at the hallway and saw that it was empty. As he left, he made sure not to create any sound that some nosey neighbor might remember if questioned. Then he slipped in his lock pick and slid the bolt shut. As he headed to the stairs, he felt satisfied with the planting of the evidence. Now it was up to the cops to make sure it was dug up.

Chapter Fourteen

Monday Afternoon

Lieutenant Newman sat his desk at PHPD headquarters feeling like ever since he became involved with Vince Singleton he should be taking movie courses instead of brushing up on police procedures. Vince had filled him in on what his film fanatic team had come up with, and he was now looking up info on *Basic Instinct* at the IMDb website. He was going to try to stream the movie this evening, if it was available, and if not, Vince would lend him his copy of the DVD.

Newman could feel Smartley closing in on his work area. The detective's stocky form displaced the air around him as he moved toward people, like a bear charging his prey.

"What the hell do you want, Smart-less?" said Newman without looking up from the desktop screen.

"A little respect, for one," said Smartley, his voice sounding like a growl. "I've been here a lot longer than you, or don't you remember?"

"Yeah, I do. I don't have early onset dementia, old-timer. Can you recall what you ate for breakfast?"

"Forget about my diet. But, the Captain might want to have you as his main meal of the day after you talk with Lieutenant Douglas, who wants to see you. Now."

Smartley walked away with a chuckle. Newman headed for Douglas' desk, wondering why he wanted to see him. Vince had contacted Douglas, so maybe he wanted to question him, given Newman's past relationship with the "victim." His cop mind prompted him to use an unemotional word because the police were supposed to be detached to do their jobs, and becoming emotionally involved blurred objectivity. But Kate was a woman with whom he was once passionately involved, and he couldn't disengage his feelings. He couldn't block out remembering her sly smiles, bright eyes, and uninhibited laughter. Those heated arguments they had were followed by fiery lovemaking. There was no way her death could not be personal.

Smartley's swaggering attitude led him to think he wasn't going to have a comfy, collaborative session with his fellow lieutenant. Douglas sat at his desk. "Sat" wasn't exactly the right word. His backside hardly touched the seat, as Douglas almost stood up as he leaned forward, focusing on his computer screen.

"Please sit down, Lieutenant," he said without looking at Newman. There was an uncomfortable period of silence before Douglas spoke.

"Please tell me when was the last time you saw Katherine Lawrence."

"People never called her 'Katherine.' She preferred the less stuffy 'Kate,' instead."

"Just answer the question, Newman."

"It was about six months ago. It was at City Hall. She was asking me about an aspect of police investigation in connection with a case she was working. Why do you ask?"

Douglas finally looked away from his computer, and confronted Newman with a clenched face.

"Are you sure about when you saw the victim?"

It was now Newman's turn to shoot off a stern look.

"Yeah, pretty damn sure. Now, are you going to tell me what the hell this is about?"

Douglas pulled an evidence bag out of a desk drawer and threw it on the table close to Newman. Inside the bag was a wrapper from one of Samantha's donuts that had "For Cops Only" written on it.

"Look, this is a sensitive situation. I don't like confronting a fellow lieutenant about being a suspect in a murder investigation. But, I thought it would be better if I handled this talk instead of one of the detectives. I was hoping you would have just said you happened to be at Lawrence's place the other day. But, now you tell me it was six months since you saw her, and I have evidence, which several police department personnel have identified as yours, and which came into your possession recently, which was found at the victim's home that directly contradicts your statement."

Newman's mind and heart started to race. *What the hell was going on here? How could his jelly donut wrapper wind up at Kate's home?*

"Lieutenant, why would the perpetrator, especially a cop, leave a piece of evidence that obviously connected him to the case? Everyone knows I am not that stupid. Someone is setting me up."

"For what purpose?"

"Look, there are certain colleagues here who were not exactly, how should I say, supportive of my working with Vince Singleton. The fellow has not ingratiated himself with the Department because of his claims that some cops may have been complicit in his wife's death. As you may know, the Captain has allowed me to investigate that possibility."

Newman paused for a second to soften his previous remarks with his next words.

"Of course, hopefully, I won't find any wrongdoing on the part of any policeman."

Douglas offered a slight grin, acknowledging Newman's attempt at diplomacy.

"You make some good points, Newman. But, I can't ignore the evidence. I could go through the paperwork of getting a warrant to search your home. However, I was hoping you would welcome the chance to exonerate yourself by welcoming us into your residence."

Newman's tight smile showed an appreciation of the attempt at professional courtesy.

"Fine. But I would like you present, to make sure the search is on the up and up. I don't keep plants in my place, so I don't want anyone bringing one along. And, no Smartley. I'm sure he was the one who wanted to lead the search of my home. That guy and me go together like the Cowboys and the Eagles."

"Done," said Douglas, letting out a short sigh of relief.

Chapter Fifteen

Tuesday Morning

Vince knew the drill at the Pullman Correctional Facility in Northeast Philadelphia. He always felt like he was going through the security line at an airport, only more so. A guard, whose stature qualified him to play the same position on an NFL offensive line, frisked Vince. He also had to open his mouth for inspection. Luckily they weren't checking any other orifices.

Even before going to the prison, security had already been on Vince's mind. He convinced Gina to stay at his house for the time being, and persuaded Hope to postpone her apartment search. Even though Douglas appreciated making it easier to protect the women, he also pointed out that placing Gina and Hope at one location made it easier for the perpetrator to get at them. This acknowledgement of the existing threat did not help to alleviate Vince's fears.

At least in this maximum-security prison he felt relieved that one of the women he knew was safe. It was not only the fact that Cassandra Kimble was incarcerated that assured him of her being harm-free. He knew from firsthand experience, that is a karate kick to the head, that she could not only take care of herself, but anyone else in the immediate area. Her adoptive father had done a good job of teaching her how to use her body, and any available weapons, to defend herself.

How could that man have known that she would have taken what he taught her to inflict instead of protect?

Vince entered the large round open room and observed the stoical guards encircling the prisoners who were seated at tables with their visitors. The gray and blue uniformed sentries did not move, looking lifeless as sharks before they attacked. He spied Cassandra seated toward the back. She rose, her tall, toned form and her raven-black ponytailed hair reminding him of her appearance when he first saw her as one of his literature students. She smiled, which given her track record with men, was not necessarily a welcome invitation. Even though he was almost one of her victims, and was the one to catch her, the two had forged a strange friendship. Their mutual love of movies, and his help in polishing her screenwriting talents, were a couple of the elements that combined to produce the amalgam that held together their relationship.

Vince approached her location and sat down at the bolted down table and chairs.

"Sorry about Kate Lawrence," he said.

Cassandra cocked her head sideways to her right and continued her sly smile.

"Grim is the reaper. But is it so surprising? An intellectual, independent, sensual woman defending the animal-loving, but man-hating killer freak. She had a lipstick drawn target on her back. I said before how you guys love your trophies, acquired through sex or violence, sometimes both."

"So, you think it was a man who did it?"

Cassandra gave out a "Ha," followed by a "No doubt."

"Faye Patterson enrolled in my Main Line Movie Academy class."

"Ah, well there is always the unevolved, jealous exception to the rule."

Vince leaned forward and spoke in a low and what he hoped was a calming tone.

"Lawrence's loss is a blow to your appeal. Are you okay?"

"Aw, he cares about me. Want to kiss the scar on my neck where you stabbed me, make it all better?" she said, batting her lengthy eyelashes.

"Now Cassandra, behave. I thought you said the therapy was working."

She laughed and waved her hand back and forth as if erasing what she said.

"Just messing with you, Mr. S. Because of you I now understand that there are those of the male persuasion who can be trusted, although there are still too few of you fellas out there."

"Do you need any help getting legal aid?"

"Hey, I'm a sideshow celebrity now. I have plenty of bling-slinging lawyers wanting to represent me, for genuine reasons, and also self-promoting selfish ones. Besides, there hasn't been an execution in Pennsylvania in ages, and the governor has put a stay on capital punishment."

She looked as if she was testing a thought in her mind.

"Do they have any leads on who killed Kate?"

"No, but I'm going to let you in on some of what I know and what I suspect."

Vince brought Cassandra up-to-date on the text he received and the evidence at the scene of the murder. When he told her about the numerous deep penetrating stab wounds the murderer inflicted on Lawrence, he saw Cassandra shudder, looking as if something cold ran through her body.

"And another shocker is that Newman called me and said there was evidence planted at Lawrence's apartment to imply that Newman was there recently. Now he's a suspect because of his past romantic relationship with her."

"Wow. This is like over-the-top," said Cassandra. "I know you're worried about the ladies in your life. But you know there are a lot of empowered women out there who have responded to our blog posts on violence against females. They all have to watch their backs."

Alarm rang through Vince.

"Yeah, you're right. Here I was just thinking of Gina and Hope. I liked it better when my profile was low. I don't want to be the one that helps get women in general hurt by rocking the gender boat."

"Can't control the aftershocks when you're shaking the earth people stand on. Let's change the subject. What did you think of the last revision of the script?"

Vince had brought Cassandra's screenplay with him and they discussed her story about outsiders, whom she called "unsocials," and several others who inherit what's left of the earth by escaping to an unaffected island after a toxic environmental event wipes out most of the world's population. Vince had to admit that it was a clever satire on the irresponsible and violent tendencies of humans versus the in-sync with nature characteristics of animals. The writing contained a large dose of venom against stereotypical male-female relationships.

They were at the end of the discussion and Vince just had a couple of final comments.

"I think if you add some signature traits, such as speech patterns, or physical gestures, to individualize the characters, and, in a few spots, use more behavior than words, it should be in good shape. I'll then pitch it to the Hollywood agent that is handling me and Vernon."

Cassandra was quiet for a second and then spoke without looking at Vince.

"I can't believe after what I have done, how I attacked you, that you would do all this for me. Thank you."

"Your welcome," was all that Vince, usually a man of many words, could come up with.

Cassandra took a deep breath before she spoke again.

"You asked me for my input about your movie course on the portrayal of women. You know, I was one of those seductive women who was lethal to the men I encountered. So, am I one of your femme fatales?"

Vince shook his head.

"Cassandra, you're not a flat literary archetype, behaving according to a predetermined set of rules. What you did was wrong, and you are being punished for your crimes. But, men abused you, warped you, sowed their demon seeds on violently susceptible soil. But there are many layers to you, Cassandra. Writing talent, caring about the rights of animals, and the desire to prevent other women from suffering what you endured, make you more than a stock character."

Cassandra shifted in her chair, rubbed her hands together, like a girl scout trying to spark something. Vince guessed she was struggling to find a way to say something to him. Vince knew it was difficult for her to show her feelings behind the tough façade she developed to protect her from more emotional scarring. When she spoke she looked directly at Vince, and he could sense that she wanted the weight of each her words to make an impression on him.

"They think I killed my adoptive father. I did think about it. I loved him for caring for me, teaching me about self-defense, trying to help me protect myself. I know now that I didn't know how to respond to that kind of fatherly love. The so-called fathers before him only used me for their – gratification. When he rejected what I thought he wanted, I assumed he rejected me. But I didn't go through with it. It really was an accident, his fall down those steps. You have to believe me."

"I do," said Vince. "I thought that when all that information came out based on your testimony and the investigating that followed, that there might have been some leniency coming your way. The men who were your targets did some vile things. I was shocked to learn about Patterson's driving that college girl he was having sex with to suicide after using her and then dumping her. Even covered up her death, making it look like an accidental drug overdose. We knew that director Sidney Foreman abused animals in his films, but it was horrible to find out that he made those underground rape fantasy movies. And David Taylor hid his collaboration with Foreman on some of those projects. Those men caused a lot of suffering."

Cassandra bowed her head.

"But it was still murder. And, I deserve my punishment."

Vince could see Cassandra finding relief in a period of silence, and then in changing the topic.

"Getting back to your affinity for sharp objects, how are your knife throwing lessons going? That fellow I connect you with working out?"

"Yeah, he's been a big help. That Ridge Runner knife set was a good call."

"I have to hand it to him. Dad knew his way around weapons. But I'd bet you a state-of-the-art prison shiv he didn't expect me to go from defense to offense with them."

Vince gave out a quick bark of a laugh.

"Who would have thought I would be pretty good at tossing cutlery?" he said.

"Me, for obvious reasons. Still, you might want to think about using something with a little more power and that covers some distance. Remember, be patriotic, buy American. I may have a coupon for a semiautomatic somewhere."

Vince was not smiling.

"I don't like guns."

Cassandra nodded her head before speaking.

"Understandable," she said. "How is Newman making out on Jewel's case?'

"He has been checking out the lists of policemen who were ordered to have counseling by the Philly Police Department. He is cross-checking those cops with the list of Jewel's clients that I gave him and is looking for any officers who may have sought her services on their own. He's trying to discover any incriminating connection to the cops, Campbell and Edmonds, to figure out why Jewel's records were stolen, and she was killed."

"Any luck so far?"

"Nada."

Cassandra thought for a minute.

"Well, Mr. S, he might want to widen his lasso. Maybe he should check out any of Jewel's patients who weren't policemen, but who knew the cops in the shooting."

Vince's raised eyebrows acted like facial exclamation points as he nodded his head at the suggestion.

Chapter Sixteen

Wednesday Morning

Lieutenant Newman was on his third cup of Folgers, and his second jelly donut. Even fellow policemen rummaging through his apartment couldn't kill his appetite. But he was anxious as hell and the caffeine and sugar didn't help his nervousness. He wished he had more time to check out his place. If someone had placed his donut wrapper at Kate's home, maybe he hid something incriminating here also. Lt. Harvey Douglas and his team arrived at 9 o'clock and had been at it for about a half hour. Newman knew he had to cooperate. If he cop-blocked the investigation, it would only make him appear more suspicious. There certainly were a lot of latex covered hands fingering his stuff. And he liked his stuff.

"Nice sports memorabilia you have here, Newman," said Douglas walking around the living room, sipping the black brew Newman served him. The rich java blend made the room smell like a diner around morning rush hour. Douglas stopped in front of Newman's 2008 World Series ticket.

"That 2008 Phillies' team had a lot of talent. Those were the days, huh?"

Newman paced around the room and looked up from his cup of coffee.

"Yeah, there definitely have been better days."

The investigative team moved quickly around the two lieutenants, making Newman feel as if he was in the eye of a forensic hurricane. They dusted for fingerprints, searched for non-matching clothing fibers, checked out the trash bins, and bagged anything they thought might contain DNA evidence. They overturned the sofa and the bed to see if anything revealing was hidden underneath. Other officers scoured the apartment for whatever looked out of place.

"Got something," called out a cop coming from the bedroom.

"What the hell ..." started Newman, sensing a sinking feeling accompanying the donuts in his stomach.

The policeman held up a small shopping bag with one hand and pulled out a woman's silk scarf with the other. He handed both to Douglas, who held the scarf in one gloved hand. He looked in the bag and fished out a small piece of paper.

"The date on this receipt is within the last month," said Douglas. "Sure looks like one of those we found at Lawrence's house."

"How do we know it's hers?" asked Newman. "It could have been bought by anyone."

"It has her initials on it. But, we'll check the store and the last four digits of the credit card number to see if she was the shopper."

"Hey, one more thing," called out an officer in the bathroom.

"This isn't happening," said Newman as he felt sweat dampening his shirt.

The policeman handed a tube of lipstick to Douglas, who twisted the bottom of the holder, revealing a pink-hued cosmetic stick.

"Your shade?" said Douglas to Newman.

"This is bullshit! You know this is a frame, right? You won't find any other evidence of Kate Lawrence in this place, no prints, no DNA. Just these two items. And, why would of all people a cop leave such incriminating evidence for you to find?"

"Good points. But I have to follow the clues."

Team members bagged the evidence and kept searching the apartment.

He turned to Newman.

"Let's head back to headquarters. I have to report to the Captain. I'm sorry, but you know there are procedures that must be put into effect."

Chapter Seventeen

Thursday Afternoon

"This is such crap!" said Vince. "How can they suspend you? These are detectives, right? Aren't they supposed to smell a frame, especially one that stinks like a politician's promises?"

As Newman sat on the brown couch in the family room, Vince looked at the death grip the lieutenant had on his mug of coffee. To Vince, it looked like Newman would have preferred squashing somebody's head with his large hands instead.

"As Douglas said, he has to follow the evidence. He knows there's something wrong. But, until he sorts it out, I can't be involved officially. So, I played the scene you have seen on many cop shows where I turned in my badge and my gun."

Vince paced around the room, as his agitated mind sought an outlet to channel his frustration. He worried that his anger might have upset Gina and Hope. He saw Gina's trance-like expression, her way of distancing herself from unpleasant talk. Hope, sitting in a lotus position on the rug, scratching a purring Jellybean, looked like she was trying to transcend the tense situation.

"Is it okay for you to be here?" asked Gina. "I mean, will the policeman out front report you, get you in trouble?"

Newman relinquished his death grip on the mug and took a sip of the dark brew.

"No, Joe out there is alright. We've worked together. Besides, if it just appears that I'm visiting with friends, they'll cut me some slack."

Even though Vince physically stopped pacing, his mind continued walking through what might happen next.

"I just feel like I'm waiting for the next text to drop, and I would feel safer if we had you watching our backs, keeping us informed. I know I can trust you, and I wish there were more people I could say that about. Well, Douglas still has to keep me in the loop. He seemed pleased with our theory about how most of the clues refer to *Basic Instinct*. But, besides limiting your helping us with this case, I'm more concerned about why someone is trying to frame you, Ray."

Hope said to Newman what Vince was also suspecting.

"Could someone inside the police force be using your connection to Lawrence to get at you? Take you, to quote my father's book title, out of the picture?"

"Could be," said Newman. "I've pissed off some cops with my quick promotion and the impression that I've betrayed fellow officers by working with a certain writer who was critical of the force's investigation into his wife's death."

Newman and Vince exchanged smiles that barely registered on the grin meter.

"It's a good bet your investigation into Jewel's death is the reason for what's happening to you," said Vince. "Which reminds me."

Vince was reluctant to mention what transpired at his visit at the prison, but he wanted them to know the source of the helpful suggestion.

"I visited Cassandra, and she brought up a good point."

Newman leaped from the couch and confronted Vince.

"Why do you continue to associate with that girl? She is a murderer who tried to kill you."

"Yeah, dad, she is one scary chick."

Vince saw in Gina's face the same apprehension expressed by Newman.

"Look, she's in prison for life for what she has done," said Vince. "But, she has gained some insights into herself, and she wants to help. Now can we just try to be objective here?"

After Newman seemed to almost visually shrink after letting off some angry steam, he sat back down on the couch.

"You have been investigating police officers that may have been involved in Jewel's death," said Vince. "Cassandra said that maybe we should look into some of Jewel's patients who weren't cops but may have been associated with someone on the force. Let's face it, the only way to get you clear of this frame and help with both Jewel's and Lawrence's cases is to step up the fight."

There was a brief period of silence as Vince watched the others consider what he told them.

"Might be worth considering," said Gina.

"Yeah, could be something there," said Hope.

Newman was more reluctant, but got on board.

"Suppose it wouldn't hurt to widen the search, since we don't have anything concrete so far."

"Yeah, I have the list of her patients, but with you on the bench how do we get back into the game?" asked Vince, as he started pacing again.

Vince saw Newman ponder the question.

"Might be time to get my father out of retirement. He still has a friend in the department, a captain. He admired my dad for not teaming up with dirty cops. Maybe because someone's after me, he may be persuaded to help out."

"Sounds promising," said Vince, "Now, if you'll excuse me, I have to get ready for my class tonight."

"Your students might be suspects in Kate's death," said Newman. "Along with your mouth, keep your eyes and ears open."

Chapter Eighteen

Thursday Evening

The temperature in the classroom was definitely more person friendly than it had been a week ago, so someone at the Main Line Movie Academy had actually responded to Vince's complaint. But, he was still perspiring slightly. The sweat was due to being in his PTSD hyperalert mode. He cursed himself for forgetting to ask that his iced white chocolate mocha be decaf at Starbucks. He could have done without the extra heart thumping. He looked around, making sure there was no one in attendance who was not enrolled in the session. He observed the class members, checking out their movements as they reached for contents in their bags.

He reluctantly dimmed the lights to show a clip from one of the films included in the night's discussion. His apprehension grew as his ability to observe his surroundings diminished. That worry only increased because of the first film he was going to discuss. He started showing the scene from *Basic Instinct* where Sharon Stone's character rides in the back of the car while the detective played by Michael Douglas sits in the front passenger seat as his partner drives. After the clip was finished and he quickly restored brightness to the room, Vince addressed his audience.

"What can we determine from this scene about the two main characters?"

The first hand that flew into the air was that of Pauline Josephs, although, in her case, again, it was a fist.

"Yes, Ms. Josephs."

"Stones' Catherine is very smart. She studied psychology and figures out that Douglas' Nick has an addictive personality. She already is wearing him down, egging him on by offering him a cigarette even after he says he has quit smoking."

"Very good," said Vince. "Since I'm assuming you all saw the film as part of your assignments, where else in the movie do we see Nick's addictive personality, and Catherine's effect on him? Mr. Goldman."

Joe Goldman was never at a loss for words when he posted comments on Vince's movie blog. But now that Vince called on him, he seemed so thrilled that he was unable to express himself in real life.

"Ah, ah, what was it that I was going to say? It had to do with his addictions. Well, of course it did. Well, we see Nick, who has tried to be sober, fall off the wagon, and start drinking again after Catherine gets under his skin."

"Good observation," said Vince. He looked around the room at the other raised hands and called on Bill Herrman.

"Obviously, Catherine is the key to unlocking Nick's sexual addiction," said Herrman. "He practically sexually assaults his ex-girlfriend, that psychologist played by Jeanne Tripplehorn, after Catherine has fired him up with her underwear-free exhibition at the police station. Poor guy can't see straight after she gets her claws into him."

Hope waved her hand so much Vince could almost feel the breeze she created.

"Okay, let's hear from Hope. This better be good, daughter."

"Stop with the parental pressure. Anyway, let's not act like Nick is any different than most guys. They are so sexually obsessed that they allow themselves to lose control of their common sense. And, as Dr. Solomon pointed out last week, since women had limited power in the past, they had to use this male weakness."

Vince felt that he had to play devil's advocate.

"Yes, in the past maybe women had only one option. But, this film deals with a modern, successful woman. Why is this character using sex to manipulate men?"

Faye Patterson called out without raising her hand.

"Because that type of woman also has a weakness. It is one of low morality. And, that kind of harpy has always existed, and is to blame for bringing about a man's destruction."

Vince knew that Faye's comments sprung from her personal story, but he used her comments to get back to the tales from the scripts.

"So, even if men may be perpetually susceptible to manipulation due to their obsession, and women may use this vulnerability, why is a movie like *Basic Instinct* different than movies like *The Natural* and *The Maltese Falcon* discussed last week which also contain the femme fatale characters?"

Vince wanted to hear from a new voice and called on Ike Lacy.

"Catherine gets away with her male-destroying crimes," Lacy said. "She is like a praying mantis, who has been known to devour the male of the species right after the sex act. Maybe we should spell 'praying' with an 'e' instead of an 'a.'"

"Nice analogy and word play, Mr. Lacy," said Vince, noting that the young man seemed more self-assured this time around. "Yes, that is one substantial difference here. But, also, remember at the beginning of the film she admits that she liked having sex with the first victim. Her enjoyment of sex is singled out here, as opposed to some other femme fatale characters. Is this a negative response given the plot, or is this a breakthrough in female sexual liberation? Dr. Solomon will now explore other films similar to *Basic Instinct*, and we will eventually deal with other stories that explore the depiction of female sexuality in movies."

Solomon took over and talked about similarities between *Basic Instinct*, *Body Heat* and *The Last Seduction*. He also talked generally about female revenge movies that showed the males as villainous sexual abusers, who were defeated by empowered women, such as *Sleeping with the Enemy* and *Enough*. After the class, some of the students approached Vince about what they heard in the news, namely his participation in another homicide investigation. Vince dreaded this part of his involvement. He had walked away from some reporters at the building's entrance and planned on exiting with Hope out the back way to go home.

"Mr. Singleton, can you tell us anything about the clues left at the Lawrence murder scene?" asked Goldman. "They obviously refer to movies, or you wouldn't be consulting on the case, right?"

"You figured that out on your own, Columbo?" said Lacy.

Goldman narrowed his eyes and glared at the source of the gibe.

"Um, sounds like somebody should be put down for his put-downs," said Josephs in a whimsical voice camouflaging the zing in her words.

"Nice to see you again, Ms. Josephs," said Lacy.

Pauline ignored Lacy.

"I do hope you can help find the person responsible for Kate Lawrence's death, Mr. Singleton. I think she was a prime example of an empowered woman, and a fighter for just causes. I'm a Penn law student and I hope to be as good an attorney as she was. It's a shame that Cassandra Kimble lost such a brilliant defense lawyer."

"Yeah, well excuse me if I don't share your sympathy for the justly jailed Cassandra," said Hope. "The chick did try to off my dad, remember?"

"And yet your father, here, has risen above that attack on him, and has seen how abusing women can only lead to more abuse, and to the warping of what could be high achieving females," responded Josephs.

Vince shifted and looked away, feeling uncomfortable about any discussion involving his personal life. Well, it was his own fault for making his private life so public.

"As to your question, Mr. Goldman, I can't discuss anything about the case, even though, as you have already concluded, there are some aspects that may refer to films. And, Ms. Josephs, thank you for your support."

Josephs gave a quick nod and smile, and headed for the exit.

Herrman and Lacy stared at the young woman's shapely legs revealed by her short skirt as she walked out of the room.

"It's like Jell-O on springs," said Lacy.

"Well some like it hot," said Herrman. "And, she certainly causes the thermometer to rise."

Vince smiled at the references to the line delivered by Jack Lemmon and the title of the Billy Wilder comedy.

"But, speaking of femme fatales, she is quite the man-eater. I was in another film class with her and there were a couple of guys in that course who she chewed up and spit out. With her you'll definitely need a bigger boat," said Lacy.

"Is that all you two are concerned about, where she registers on the sex-counter?" asked Hope. "How about the fact that she is intelligent and articulate?"

"Wait a minute," said Herrman, "you just dissed her for giving the Kimble gal a like."

"Never heard of shades of gray?" said Hope. "Can't deal with a little complexity, huh? When men become involved with many women it's like they wear a victory badge. But when women date around, it's like guys want to pin the scarlet letter on them. I'll tell ya.' The never-ending double S."

Herrman flashed an appealing large grin.

"When you're right, you're right," he said. "Pardon me. I'm only a man. Nobody's perfect."

"Hey, I should have said that line," said Lacy. "I'm the one who started the *Some Like it Hot* thread."

"Time for us to go," said Vince. He smiled to himself, because it was usually Hope rescuing him from verbal confrontations. He gently directed her toward the back entrance.

"See you, Mr. Singleton," Lacy called out to the retreating Vince. "Thanks for getting the A/C fixed."

Vince waved his "You're welcome."

Chapter Nineteen

Friday Morning

Lieutenant Newman wasn't used to having a weekday morning off from work, even in the summertime when all you wanted to do was enjoy warm temperatures and long sunlit days. He had only taken a couple of one-week vacations since he had joined the police force, and he usually went to where his family would get away from it all when he was young – the not-so-distant Ocean City, New Jersey. The shore town had changed a great deal since his youth, with the old awning-draped, cedar-sided buildings replaced by modern high-priced low-maintenance homes. But, he still liked walking along the beach or the boardwalk, eating slices of Manco's pizza followed by Kohrs Brothers soft-serve ice cream. He also would wander off the boardwalk onto Asbury Street to check out the new stores there, maybe picking up a large chocolate chip cookie along the way.

He might have been thinking about vacations, but he didn't want a permanent one. So, he was at his father's house just off of Rhawn Street in the Northeast part of Philadelphia, where his parents had moved a few years before his mother's death, to talk to his dad about getting his son back on active duty. He brought along cups of black coffee and donut holes, knowing how much his pop loved the combo. However, he felt a bit guilty, knowing he was contributing to the old man's expanding waistline.

Pete Newman opened the door after the knocks and greeted his expected son's visit with a smile after seeing the goodies his boy held up in front of him.

"You're a good cop, bringing donut treats to a fellow policeman," said Pete.

"Well, maybe a good cop, but maybe a not-so-good son, adding to your cholesterol count," said Newman. "But, you didn't say 'retired' policeman, so I'm hoping you decided to temporarily be back on the job."

The two sat down at the kitchen table which still had last night's dirty dishes on it. Newman noticed that his dad saw his son look at the remains of the prior day and issued a command.

"Don't even think about cleaning up."

Newman held up his hands in surrender. As his dad sipped the black coffee and popped a couple of the glazed doughy desserts into his mouth, Newman realized he may be looking at a senior version of himself in 35 years, equipped with an older version of the same hawkish face and crew cut head of hair.

"Of course I'll do what I can to help," said Pete between chews. "Fred Danson knows I showed him the ropes when he became my partner after getting out of the Academy. Good thing I got him to be reassigned though, before he could catch my heat. At least I had a part in getting an honest guy to rise through the ranks. There's something to be said for that."

Newman also sampled a couple of the sweets. He again thought how unfair it was that his father, who never informed on anybody, was accused by fellow cops of ratting them out in an Internal Affairs investigation of crooked policemen just because he refused to be on the take.

"There are more clean cops than you think, Dad, especially the younger ones. But I could use an established one with some clout to help me out with the Singleton case."

Pete Newman wiped his hands sideways against each other to remove some of the sugary coating.

"Okay. What do you need."

"Well, if I hit a crooked nerve in the department working on Jewel Singleton's cold case and somebody is trying to set me up, then solving that case will help get me healthy again."

Newman stopped to take a gulp of his strong brew before continuing.

"I was striking out just looking for cops associated with Jewel Singleton. There was a suggestion that maybe she was killed because someone she saw professionally was involved with a policeman. Vince gave me a list of his wife's patients. I've been frozen out of the police database, so I need someone to see if one of these names jives with a badge."

Pete looked at the bags under his boy's eyes.

"You hanging in there, sport? Looks like the weight you're carrying is starting to lay you low."

Newman smiled at his father's concern.

"I'll be alright. Douglas said he'll work on keeping my name out of the press as being a possible suspect in the Lawrence case. That should ease things a bit."

Pete patted his son on the shoulder.

"I'll do everything I can to help you get out of this mess."

Chapter Twenty

Late Friday Afternoon

Vince's increasing annoyance with things now spread to himself. He had not needed a counseling session in a while, since both his professional and private lives were doing much better. But now that this new threat loomed over those he cared about, his post-traumatic stress disorder symptoms reemerged. He was upset with himself for not being able to control his condition after using the tools his therapy had taught him. So, here he was at Dr. Michael Probst's office for a session, just as he promised Hope.

Vince stared out at the Philadelphia skyline through the large window next to Probst's desk. The view usually had a calming effect on his mind, providing a sense of supernatural soaring above the human problems festering below. Today, he could not achieve that healing feeling of distance.

"So, not doing so great, Vince?" asked Probst.

"What a negative life you lead. You only get to see people on their off days."

"Not so. Sometimes I have a patient come in and say he or she has turned it around, life is great, and thanks me for helping out."

Vince looked at Probst's overly cheerful face.

"Yeah, that doesn't happen too often, does it?"

"No, not really," said the psychologist. "Usually when they are doing well, they just disappear and I don't get to hear the nice stories. I sort of invent happy endings for them."

"Maybe you should be a fiction writer," said Vince, as he scrutinized Probst's face. "I just noticed that you look a bit like Alan Arkin when he played Freud in *The Seven-Per-Cent Solution*?"

"Does that mean I come off more like an actor than a real psychoanalyst? Couldn't you have at least compared me to someone handsome, like Sidney Poitier's prison psychiatrist in *Pressure Point*?"

"You should be so lucky to look that good. But, a nice reference to a great movie that was underappreciated. An incisive study of the roots of fascism, and how it can spread when we blame a group of people for all of the ills of others."

"Just to put you at ease, as a patient, you don't resemble Bobby Darin in that film."

"Thank goodness. He was one scary neo-Nazi. Not as frightening as the real ones, though."

Probst cleaned his eyeglasses before speaking again.

"So, Vince, any problems you want to discuss?"

"Yes. Guilt. And I don't blame it on anyone else. Only me."

Probst offered a slight reassuring smile.

"I know your visit has to do with you becoming involved in the Kate Lawrence murder investigation. I'm not sure it was wise getting mixed up in that given your history, but I admire you for trying to help out. So, you shouldn't feel guilty about experiencing PTSD symptoms. We can work on that. And, you know what I'm going to say about guilt."

"Sure. Guilt is an anchor which only holds you back. Own it, but don't let it stop you from moving forward with a plan to avoid repeating prior setbacks."

"Wow. I guess I've done my job really well. I could have used this hour to play Candy Crush."

"Not so fast. The problem here is a little more complex and can't be solved by a plug-in answer."

Probst leaned forward and stared at Vince with microscopic grey eyes.

"Okay, we'll cut the banter. What's the deal?"

Vince took a deep breath and let out a slow cleansing exhalation to rid himself of the pain of having to discuss his feelings.

"I didn't volunteer. I was drafted."

Vince, secure in the fortress of doctor-patient confidentiality, told Probst about the text from the murder suspect.

"So, I'm not just upset with myself about my inability to get a handle on my symptoms. The real problem is my ego which propelled me into wanting to solve Cassandra Kimble's murders, and then drove me toward seeking praise for my writing. That unbridled pride made me a magnet which drew in a sociopath who threatens those I love, and maybe others. Ironically, my love of movies may have turned a personal passion into something poisonous to those around me."

Probst waived his hand quickly from left to right as if to dismiss Vince's demons.

"Cassandra read your novel about misunderstood outsiders. She was one of those fringe people, and it brought her to you. This killer may fit into that pattern. But, true artists can't second-guess their creative process by worrying about all the possibilities that might happen by those experiencing their creativity. If they did, Alfred Hitchcock would probably have worked for Walt Disney."

The line elicited a slight "ha" from Vince, but he felt his sadness quickly returning.

"It was better when I was a nobody, getting only involved in my own drama. But, no, I had to grandstand it, seeking understanding for the man-killing Cassandra. And then going online with posts about abuse of women. Instead of getting something accomplished, all I did was stir up the crazy pot."

Probst shook his head.

"Don't cause-and-effect yourself into the mental ward. People who fight to make the world better have to expose the evil. Unfortunately, they also expose themselves to that evil. It takes courage and commitment to go down that road."

Probst paused. He leaned toward Vince and grasped his wrist.

"You didn't seek what happened before, but once you arrived there, you worked to make things right. Unfortunately, you are being forced to play that role again. I'll do my best behind the scenes to help you."

Vince stared at the city on the other side of the window.

"Okay, Doc. But, you may be working overtime."

Chapter Twenty-one

Sunday Night

It was just as easy with Pauline Josephs as it had been with the Lawrence woman. The sedative again worked quickly after the injection just inside the vestibule of the Spruce Street apartment building. It wasn't far from the center for abused women where Josephs finished her weekly Sunday evening volunteer work. That activity followed her usual partying on Saturday evening with her twenty-something friends. The predator observed her recently at the clubs she frequented where her scant clothing attracted numerous males whom she rejected until she chose the one for the night to reward. *The next day the fellow was castrated from her memory,* thought the killer.

The murderer placed the shapely woman's body on the black leather couch in the living room of her apartment, while noting with aversion how cluttered the place was. The attacker replaced her jeans and tank top with a short, form-fitting dress, and rolled dark thigh-high stockings up her slender, smooth legs. To the humming of "Stand by Your Man," the killer looked around the room and was happy to discover an appropriate object on a bookcase shelf filled with DVD's. It was a snow globe which contained a sled with the words "Rosebud" written on it, referencing the film *Citizen Kane*. The vinyl, latex, and plastic apparel were worn again, and the globe was then used to bludgeon Josephs to death. The murderer placed a wig with long wavy blonde hair over the short-haired girl's head as the blood dripped down her face. Just as with Kate Lawrence, the death had to be, unfortunately, messy.

After placing the other items, it was time for the text to Singleton and the call to the police.

Chapter Twenty-two

One AM Monday Morning

Vince Singleton couldn't sleep. And, he didn't want to. The rest his body craved was like contaminated food that caused him to regurgitate unwanted memories. When he did drift off, he relived Jewel's murder and the investigation into the deaths of Cassandra's victims. But, his awake state provided no relief since the waking nightmare of this current threat haunted his conscious mind.

While Hope slept in her room and Gina was asleep in his, Vince sat in his brown recliner in the family room with Jellybean in his lap, who provided some comfort with her hypnotic purring. He had lowered his adjustable bed before leaving his bedroom since Gina sometimes complained of a stiff neck because of the inclined setting. Vince used the raised position to reduce the chances of experiencing nocturnal gastric reflux. His father developed esophageal cancer and Vince was paranoid since inheriting his dad's heartburn problem. Why he had this malady and his brother Jake had no digestive problems vexed Vince. He knew Jake would have said it was nurture over nature. Vince was the worrier, always analyzing, second-guessing everything. Jake seemed to instinctively follow his humanitarian, rebellious path. Vince most of the time wound up on the same road, but only after a number of challenging detours. He wondered if the inspiration for his novel, *The Different Drummer*, came more from

Jake than from himself. Of course it was that book that had drawn Cassandra to him. Another wave of guilt flowed over Vince. *Why do I even write anything at all?* he pondered.

He tuned in Turner Classic Movies and had Alfred Hitchcock's *Suspicion* playing in the background of his attention as his cerebral faculties scanned over the clues left by Kate Lawrence's killer. What were those pajamas doing on the bed? Why did the killer not use a dress to match the one worn by Sharon Stone in *Basic Instinct?* He refocused on *Suspicion* to provide some relief from his feverish questioning. But, instead, the Hitchcock movie reminded him how difficult it is to know whether someone is guilty or innocent.

His cell phone buzzed, telling Vince he received a message. He had left the device on 24/7 in case he received another text, but he also dreaded getting another communication. His apprehension now rose exponentially as he dutifully, though reluctantly, reached for his Android cell. As he did so, he felt a gush of digestive juices rising upward, despite the medications he had taken to block the acid. He rose from the chair, causing Jellybean to jump for cover. His hand trembled slightly as he entered his password and read the text:

"Hello Vince. Nice conversing with you again. Just another heads-up that you will again be dealing with your favorite people, the police. Yes, I'm sorry, but you're guilty of not being able to protect another one of your women. You don't have to move from your chair to still win the game, if you're smart enough. Of course, if you don't let me know about your progress, the truth is that there will be consequences. Nice how we can all profit from these little chats. And, like before, why don't you give Lt. Newman a shout."

Vince threw the phone onto the couch and yelled out, "Bastard!" several times as he paced through the house. Gina heard him and came out of the bedroom pulling a thin robe on as she entered the living room. Hope, squinty-eyed, also appeared.

"What's the rumpus?" said Hope, her voice sounding raspy.

"God, she is my daughter. She quotes *Miller's Crossing*, and she isn't even awake yet. Well, let me tell you something, these damned movies have gotten us into this mess!"

"What happened, Vince?" asked Gina in a soothing tone as she stroked Vince's right arm.

Vince took a couple of deep breaths and closed his eyes, as if trying to prevent all of his composure from escaping. His mind recaptured some of his calm before he told them to follow him. They went into the family room and he showed them the text. The women temporarily muted themselves, as if wanting some distance from the story playing out in in front of them. Hope was the first to speak.

"He's taunting you with movie references."

"Yes, and ones about games. It's all a big game, only it's a deadly one. That's why the allusion to *The Last of Sheila*."

"I don't understand," said a perplexed Gina. Vince pointed a hand to Hope to explain as he paced around the room.

"In *The Last of Sheila*, show biz types are invited aboard a rich producer's yacht. He shows them that he knows about their dirty little secrets by incorporating them into murder mystery game playing. He says that 'If you're smart enough' you won't have to leave your chair to figure out who the pretend murderer is. But, a real murder takes place, and –"

112

"And, the game becomes deadly," said Vince. "Our murderer is saying we are also playing a dangerous game. He's emphasizing that scary feeling with the reference to the old TV game show, "Truth or Consequences," threatening me if I don't continue to cooperate."

"And, the 'we can all profit from these little chats' line is from *The Natural*," said Hope.

"Oh yeah, I saw that one," said Gina. "Baseball is the national pastime, a benevolent game. But, in that movie, there is death, cheating, and intimidation. The line is delivered by a gangster. What was his name? Oh yeah, Gus, played by Darren McGavin. He's trying to get Robert Redford's Roy Hobbs to throw a playoff game."

They all thought for a moment, and Gina announced what they were all thinking.

"This person is no dummy."

"A smart murderer. The worst kind," said Vince. "He's killed someone else, and we didn't have an idea as to who it was! I'd like to kick this guy in his texticles!"

"That pun may not fit. It could be a woman," said Hope.

"Yeah, well, a foot to the groin doesn't have to be gender specific."

Gina sat down on the couch and held the cell phone in one hand and formed a fist with the other. Vince could see that she was angry, and he preferred that emotion to fear.

"This killer doesn't know about Newman being a suspect, and off the case, or there wouldn't be a mention about contacting him again," said Gina. "It shows that whoever is framing our lieutenant is not the one doing these murders."

Vince looked at her and confirmed her conclusion by nodding his head.

"You should call Newman anyway," said Hope. "And, you better contact Lieutenant Douglas."

Chapter Twenty-three

Five AM Monday Morning

Lt. Harvey Douglas was on alert as to any homicides reported as soon as he received the call from Vince Singleton. After the officer who took an anonymous tip about Pauline Josephs informed the lieutenant, Douglas called Singleton once he learned the victim's name to find out if he knew her. The shaken teacher confirmed that she was a member of his current film class, and answered some questions as to why Singleton thought the killer targeted her. Singleton offered that she spoke highly of Kate Lawrence's work on behalf of Cassandra Kimble. He told Singleton he would talk with him when he knew more. After he hung up he wondered if there would be more of Singleton's "women" that Douglas, too, couldn't "protect."

Douglas hustled himself to the young woman's apartment. He wasn't really a morning person, and it was way too early to be even called morning. He liked staying up late at night, watching TV or reading so that he could let his taut mind unwind from the tension of the day. He was usually dim-eyed and slack-tailed at the day's break. But, he wanted to be among the first of his law enforcement team at the location. He wasn't sure what was going on with the evidence involving Newman in the Lawrence murder, but it didn't smell right to his experienced nose, and he wanted to follow everything this time from the starting gate to insure there would be no tampering with the crime scene.

He already noted the assortment of clothing and items close to Joseph's crumpled body displayed on the leather couch. Douglas had ordered a forensics photographer to go in first with just himself as an observer to take pictures of every inch of the place. That way, Douglas would have a visible record against which to check for any unwanted manipulation of the evidence. As the photographer did his job, Douglas pulled the girl's driver's license photo from her purse. It showed Josephs to have short hair, so he knew that she now wore a blonde wig with long hair over her battered head. The killer made sure to let them know he had placed the dark nylons and tight, short skirt on the girl, since the sales tags were still on the clothes items. Because the murderer had not sexually assaulted Lawrence, Douglas guessed that the lab results would come up with the same findings here as at the Lawrence murder scene. Douglas just shook his head, partially in bewilderment, and also in dread, when he looked at the other objects. A toy red corvette was parked on the young lady's stomach. There was a legal document, that turned out to be a fake, rolled up in her right hand. It stated that Josephs left all her worldly belongings to "The American Society of Prostitutes." But, on the phony will her first name was spelled backwards. The fingers of her left hand curled around a canister of Mace. A DVD case for the film *Hush ... Hush Sweet Charlotte* sat between her right arm and the side of her torso. On the floor, next to the couch, was a gasoline can with a lighter tied to the handle.

As Douglas concentrated on watching the forensics team do their jobs, he was distracted by the tank-like advance of burly Detective Ben Smartley, whom he had failed, successfully, to provide an early invitation to the investigation.

"Lieutenant, may I ask why I wasn't called at home about this crime? I was lead detective on the Lawrence case, and since this one appears related, I think I should have been among the first on the scene."

Douglas took a sip of black coffee which he knew would only slightly get him ready for the day's dawn.

"Sorry, Detective. Informing you somehow just didn't make it to the top of my to-do list."

Douglas could see that Smartley was so steamed he could almost see the heat building up under his collar. But, the detective held, or more precisely, almost swallowed his tongue, to choke off any insubordinate remark. Douglas then filled him in on Singleton's text, the anonymous call, and the follow-up talk with Vince. Smartley looked at the victim and the area around the couch.

"I see we again have some interesting clues left for us. Since the two cases appear to be related, has there been an attempt to find out Lt. Newman's location?" asked Smartley.

"You went there awfully quickly," said Douglas, who was one step, and he hoped to be many more, ahead of the detective. "Yes, we contacted Newman. He was at his girlfriend's place and says he was having a phone conversation with his father during the probable time of death. Newman's father confirmed the telephone call. We'll also check the phone records to verify his story."

"Beg pardon, Lieutenant," said Smartley, "but Newman's name was again mentioned in the text according to what you said. Maybe he has a partner in these crimes. Even though the two of them worked together, Newman is not happy about Singleton's support of Cassandra Kimble, and probably not thrilled that his ex defended her. Don't forget the evidence showed Newman recently involved with the lawyer, including the DNA test that indicated the lipstick in Newman's apartment belonged to Lawrence. Now we have another woman dead who liked Lawrence for fighting for the Kimble bitch. Hey, maybe Newman is jealous of all the credit Singleton received for catching Kimble."

Douglas thought it sounded as if Smartley had given way too much thought about how to implicate Newman.

"A lot of 'maybe's' there, Detective," said Douglas. "Why would Newman's accomplice mention his name in the texts? Wouldn't that draw attention to him needlessly?"

"Could just be trying to throw us off. Common knowledge that Newman and Singleton teamed up before. Also, maybe the play is to make it look like the texter doesn't know Newman is off the case."

Considering how prepared this guy is, he's making a boy scout seem lax, thought Douglas.

"Let's just work the case step by step and see where it leads us, instead of us leading the case."

Douglas took another gulp of the strong coffee.

"Well, I am going to run what we found here so far by Singleton, see if any of it adds up for him, movie-wise."

"Do we have to keep cozying up to a civilian, sir? Just doesn't seem like the professional thing to do."

Douglas smiled at Smartley's pandering to his boss' dislike of collaborating with outsiders.

"Don't have a choice," said Douglas. "The killer's made sure of that."

Chapter Twenty-four

5 PM Monday Evening

Vince threatened to eat the shrimp and broccoli in the plate in front of him, his fingers pointing the fork at the Asian food. But, he gave the dish a temporary pardon, and rested his right hand on the dining room table. Gina was doing more poking than eating her pork lo mein, and even Hope, who loved the take-out from their favorite local Chinese restaurant, The Golden Noodle, had only sampled her sweet and sour chicken.

Vince had taken his acid blocker medication, but his heartburn seemed to have done an end run around the digestive defensive line. His symptoms kicked into high gear after Douglas told him the victim was Pauline Josephs. How could it be that this bright young woman would not be able to enjoy life and help others, as she clearly wanted to do? The guilt he expressed to Probst blanketed him now, carrying the stench of a death shroud that his actions had woven. His volunteering to help with his friend Stanford Patterson's murder and his subsequent writings had dominoed into a new game of death. A game he didn't want to be part of, but which he helped to initiate.

"I guess I should just Tupperware this food," said Hope. "Maybe we should watch *The Hunger Games* so we could appreciate having tasty cuisine around."

Vince only gave a faint smile as he helped his daughter and Gina clean up. Jellybean jumped up on the kitchen counter extension that skirted the dining area. She purred loudly, so Vince fed her a couple of the shrimp, which she sucked up like a furry vacuum cleaner. *At least someone in the family still has an* appetite, he thought. They went into the family room and Hope surfed the premium cable stations to put something distracting on in the background. They all sat on the couch, including Jellybean, who jumped onto Vince's lap, somehow feeling that closeness created consolation.

Hope settled on *Sleepless in Seattle*. The self-acknowledged "chick flick," (Tom Hanks even uses the phrase in the film, although he's talking about *An Affair to Remember*, which the plot *Sleepless* at times mirrors), was one Vince enjoyed, mainly because it was written by Nora Ephron, who scripted one of his favorites, *When Harry Met Sally* ... As he half-concentrated on the movie, he knew he wouldn't get much rest tonight. Instead of Seattle, it would be more like sleepless in Whitemarsh Township. Not much point in even putting on his pajamas ...

Then it hit him like a synaptic smack across his brain.

He bolted out of the sofa, startling the leaping Jellybean, and shouted at Hope.

"Turn it off!"

"Geez, I thought you liked this flick," said Hope as she fumbled with the remote.

"The pajamas found on the bed at Kate Lawrence's home. We said they didn't fit in with *Basic Instinct*. That's because they don't. Remember how we said the killer might be leaving clues pointing to the next murder? Well we were right!"

"What? What do you mean?" asked an excited Gina.

Vince took a breath.

"Pajamas are also called 'pj's.' Which happen to correspond to the first letters in Pauline Joseph's first and last names."

After a pause accompanied by a gasp, Hope said, "Holy halibut."

Vince started to pace as he spoke.

"We have to go over the clues from the second crime scene so we can predict who the next victim will be."

"Yeah, but we have to figure out how the clues fit together before we know what doesn't fit," said Hope.

Gina rubbed her chin in contemplation.

"Maybe we need the movie geeks again. It helped last time. We can start texting to see if everyone can be here tomorrow morning."

Vince knew he had a scrunched look on his face like he had sucked down lemon juice.

"After what's happened I don't want to deal with texts except when I have to. Besides the ones from the killer, I have been getting messages from tons of people, along with emails, offering their opinions on what happened to Kate Lawrence. I knew once this situation went public, it would be like, release the crackpots."

"Only fair pun on 'kraken'" said Hope.

"I'm stressed. Best I can do," said Vince. "It's not until you have to deal with so many people who invite themselves into your life do you realize the attraction of being a hermit."

Hope shrugged.

"It's the social network era."

"I'd pay good money for someone to log me out," said Vince.

Gina waved her arms like a referee interrupting play.

"Okay, okay. Hope and I will text, James, Mark, Evan, and Vernon. What about Jake?

Vince considered, and said, "Might as well. He'd be pestering me about what's going on anyway once the new news gets out. And, let's get Newman over here, too. I want him in the loop, even if it is unofficial."

"You'd better let Douglas now about the pajamas clue," said Gina.

"Right. Then I want some peaceful time for contemplation. I need this place to be like a silent movie before the talking starts."

Chapter Twenty-five

10 AM Tuesday Morning

Vince rubbed his closed eyes pointlessly, hoping to wipe away the bloodshot appearance under his lids. He was on his second cup of black coffee, decaf – he just couldn't handle how the straight stuff made him jittery – hoping its bitterness would jolt him into the task at hand. His wish for a restful sleep was futile given how events acted like triggers discharging his PTSD symptoms. Imagined violent images of Pauline Josephs now joined the actual one of Jewel in his nightmares. Would this real-life horror movie in which he played a part ever end?

The group of people already assembled in his family room were a fairly somber, quiet bunch. Gina had brought in extra chairs from the dining room area, although some of the younger visitors, including James Player and Evan Solomon sat on the floor. Mark Goodner joined Hope on the couch with Jellybean nestled in his lap. Vince figured his cat knew which one was the future veterinarian and was marking her territory. Vince saw Mark holding his daughter's hand, and he was grateful that she had someone as caring as his former college student to comfort her yet again.

Vernon Solomon tried to keep himself preoccupied by perusing Vince's bookshelves. A surprise guest was Samantha Hoffman whom Lt. Newman had invited. They sat on two seats in front of the wide screen TV, and Gina was talking with them. The lieutenant seemed grim, and had not spoken to Vince since he arrived.

Vince was becoming impatient, waiting for the usually late arrival of Jake. When he did arrive, his brother voiced his usual reporter's excuses about being delayed because of a story he was investigating. He had graduated from breaking news stories to multiple - part investigative journalism pieces.

"I apologize," he said as he dashed into the kitchen for a cup of hot brew. "I was on the phone with the state senator who keeps trying to restrict voting rights because of bogus claims of voter fraud."

Vince's reemerging PTSD irritability did not want to be restrained.

"Yeah, you're trying to replace St. Jude as the patron saint of lost causes. As the Book of Ecclesiastes says, there's nothing new under the sun. Democracy has been taken out of our hands for a long time now. So, instead of fighting lost causes, how about helping on one that can actually be won."

There was embarrassed quiet for a short time before Hope spoke.

"Dad, don't blow up the bridge that you two have built. Both of you must continue to work together."

"Vague reference to *The Bridge on the River Kwai*," whispered James to Mark, who replied with a low guttural, "Not now!"

"You're letting the current situation take control of you, stopping you from handling your symptoms," said Jake. "Remember, I have the same condition, even though it was due to combat and not loss of family. Come on, you've resumed your fight against injustices, trying to protect animals and women. Don't forget, I'm not the enemy."

"Then, who are you?" asked Vince, with a smirk on his face, letting his brother know he was calming down.

"Okay, I just walked into another movie reference. I can feel it," said his brother.

James jumped in before the rest.

"Hello, it's from *Michael Clayton* ..."

Evan interrupted, his dissertation skills already in high gear.

"Yes, and the line goes to the heart of the film. Clayton is a morally compromised lawyer and his friend, Tom Wilkinson's character, a legal partner, who now hates his role in defending a corporation accused of environmental homicide, wants to know where Michael stands."

Vernon gave his son a literal pat on the back.

"Since we now have entered the realm of movie geekdom, why don't you fill everyone in, Dad," said Hope.

Vince told the group about the clues at Pauline Joseph's place: her body, with its bashed head, found on her couch; the toy red corvette; blonde wig with long hair; the dark nylons and tight, short skirt; the fake will with Pauline's name spelled backwards; the can of Mace; the gasoline can with attached lighter; and the DVD of *Hush ... Hush Sweet Charlotte*. He related that he had a conversation with Lt. Douglas, who said they would be withholding disclosure of the DVD. Vince also told the group about the "pj" clue at the first crime scene pointing to the initials of the killer's next victim.

"It's like way too déjà vu to have another weirdo movie obsessed murderer going at it again," said Mark. "Too bad we can't Denzel it and stop this stuff from ever happening."

Vince saw the confused looks on the unobsessed film people.

"You want to translate for the non-nerdy visitors, Hope."

Hope cleared her throat before explaining.

"In the flick *Déjà Vu* Denzel Washington's law enforcement character discovers that the government has found a way to literally view recent past events."

"Like, on a very wide-screen TV," said James.

"Right," said Hope. "Sort of a video time travel thing. But, Denzel actually gets the techy people to insert him into their viewer thingie and he goes back in time to try and stop a murder and a terrorist attack."

Vince tried to get them back on track.

"Since we can't stop past crimes, let's try to prevent future ones."

Samantha Hoffman got up from her seat and walked over to where Gina was sitting, and even though she talked to her in a low voice, Vince could still hear her words.

"While these movie maniacs hash it out, I want to suggest something over another cup of coffee."

The two went into the kitchen, while the others started to talk.

"There is a red corvette driven by Gary Sinise's character in *Apollo 13*, who was grounded for fear he would contract the measles, which he didn't," said James. "But that film is way too PG for our purposes."

"There's arson and killing in *Backdraft*. We have a gas can and lighter left at Pauline Joseph's place," said Mark.

"People, come on!" said an annoyed Hope. "These killings have to do with women, and probably are ones that might be discussed in my dad's Main Line Movie Academy class."

"Um, well, I'm not sure if this will help," said Vernon, "but, the phony will could refer to *Klute*. We were going to talk about that film in detail in the class. The beneficiary in the document being, the ah, what was it, "The American Society of Prostitutes," would fit in with the clue."

Vince thought for a second, then spoke.

"Maybe. If the killings are associated with anger toward women's sexuality, then the story would fit. Jane Fonda's Bree Daniels is a prostitute and the murderer is a man who loathes women in her profession and punishes them. But, Daniels is not a powerful exploiter of men, as is Sharon Stone's character in *Basic Instinct*."

"And, Jane Fonda's hair was dark and cut in a shag in that film. Also, as best as I can recall, none of the other evidence is consistent with what happens in that movie," said Evan.

The so far silent, brooding Newman soared out of his chair like an ignited rocket.

"You people and your movies! You just try to outdo one another playing trivia. All I know, Vince, is that you seem to draw fringe lunatics, who create body counts. And now you make nice with a homicidal woman who even tried to off you. And that has brought in another wacko, and the killing continues. And for my help, I get set up for murder. Maybe the best thing to do is to stay away from you."

Samantha ran into the room and took Newman by the hand.

"Come on baby. Try to calm down," she said to the lieutenant. She led him to the door, and said to the others, "We're going to leave now. Gina, I'll be in touch."

After the two left, Gina could see how shaken Vince was by the outburst, and walked over to him, rubbing his shoulders.

"He's right," said Vince. "I'm like the goddamn angel of death."

Gina continued to rub Vince's upper back and repeated what Probst had said, that he couldn't have known Cassandra would act as she did, and it was not possible for him to have foreseen that his novel would attract such aberrant behavior from a psychologically disturbed person. And, she offered, that he couldn't control what the effects his celebrity from writing *Out of the Picture* would have on some warped person, or how an individual will react to his desire to help Cassandra and other women who have been abused.

"Like I'm not thrilled with you helping crazy Cassandra," said Hope. "But, you shouldn't blame yourself for speaking out for a good cause. And, Newman shouldn't blame you since he was the one who volunteered to find out what happened to mom. You know, Truman was right – if you can't stand the heat, get out of the kitchen."

Vince had lowered his head and held it with his hands as the others spoke. But, Hope's use of the former Commander-in-Chief's words caused him to snap to mental attention.

"Heat!" he said. "William Hurt's character drove a red Corvette in *Body Heat*, a film we were covering in the class and which definitely fits in with revenge against a woman who victimizes men, like *Basic Instinct*. The movie starts with a fire and later in the story Hurt's character, Racine, starts a fire at an abandoned beachfront hotel to make it look like the husband of the character played by Kathleen Turner was trying to commit arson. That's why the killer placed a gasoline can and lighter next to Pauline Josephs."

"Holy horseradish!" said Hope. "And Turner had long flowing blonde hair in the movie. That explains the wig on Josephs."

James was next to contribute.

"Hello, Hurt's character is a lawyer, and there is a whole plot line about his making a mistake on a will which leads to Turner's character inheriting her husband's wealth. That's why the fake will at the crime scene. The reference to prostitutes is a slam against Turner's femme fatale. She gets Hurt's character Racine to kill her husband and then frames Racine."

Vernon was next to chime in.

"Well, the, ah, the killer struck the unfortunate Ms. Josephs' head, just as Racine did with the husband in *Body Heat*, played by Richard Crenna."

"You know," said Mark, "Some of the clues that didn't fit *Basic Instinct* at Kate Lawrence's place jive with the second film. Lawrence had on a long, flowing dress like Turner's, not Stone's. And, wasn't the apartment very warm? The killer was referencing *Body Heat* by jacking up the thermostat."

Vince smiled and nodded his head.

"You're all being a big help here. But, now we have to figure out what doesn't fit? As far as I can remember, the women in *Body Heat* didn't wear dark stockings and short, tight skirts."

Mark looked at Hope, who shook her head. Vernon glanced at Evan, who shrugged his shoulders. James looked at Vince and said, "I've got nothing."

"And what about the Mace, and the DVD of *Hush ... Hush Sweet Charlotte*?" asked Gina. "It's the only time a film title is part of the evidence."

The others looked at each other, but only Vince spoke up.

"*Charlotte* has murders in it, and women commit them, but men aren't the only victims in the film. It doesn't have the "fatal female" theme that the other two movies possess. Also, I don't see any clues referring to its story. Does anybody else?"

The others shook their heads.

"There's another thing, that, ah, sort of, well bothers me. Maybe nothing," said Vernon. "The husband in *Body Heat* was knocked to the floor. Josephs was found on her couch."

Vince didn't think of that, and wasn't sure it meant anything. But, Vernon was good at picking out details.

"If the killer is consistent, some of these unfitting clues could point to another movie, and the next victim."

There was a short silence before James spoke up.

"Guess it's back to the storyboards."

Chapter Twenty-six

8 PM Tuesday Evening

Vernon Solomon wished he could give Evan a transfusion of well-being at this difficult moment in his son's life. However, he realized that his own personality had only recently developed enough of the attribute for himself, so he wasn't sure if he was the right person for donating reassurance. But, he was the father, so he would have to do the best he could.

"Evan, things have changed. We, ah, no longer live in the world of, well, when the attitudes shown in films such as *The Detective, The Best Man, and Advise and Consent* were prevalent. Look at all the movies and TV shows that now show being gay is just another acceptable lifestyle in our society. Look at the changes in the laws, bestowing rights to same-sex couples. You will be accepted for who you are."

Evan, sitting on the couch in his father's house, tugged at the collar on his shirt and then ran his fingers over the material of his pants, as if trying to maintain the pleats in the fabric.

"We think we've come a long way. But, when you get into the lives of everyday people, you still hear the giggles, and the sideways looks. I saw a swastika keyed onto the side of a car in a movie theater parking lot. Women are still viewed as sexual objects by the way they are expected to dress, whether it's on TV or at the mall. I still hear racial slurs when there is news about crime in the cities. In the dorm at college, openly gay guys were still ridiculed. One student I knew had "Fag Room – Don't turn your back on this guy" carved into his door."

He paused and looked apprehensive, which was something Vernon seldom saw his son openly exhibit.

"I'm just not sure I'm ready to talk to her about this matter," the young man said. "She hasn't really caught up to what's going on when it comes to current events. You know how she's made negative comments before. Like, whenever we watch a show where there is a romantic scene between two guys or two women, she turns her head away and says how it seems unnatural to her. I don't think she'll even talk to me again once she finds out her son, to her mind, is an aberration."

Vernon sat down on the sofa next to his boy and squeezed his arm, as if trying to remind him of the strength Evan already possessed if he just sought it out. He thought about what a rough time he and Evan's mother went through. Vernon's own insecurities and lack of self-confidence made him morbid, negative and withdrawn. Susan sought comfort elsewhere with a man who seemed the opposite of her husband, the successful academic David Taylor. Vince became even more despondent, lost his job, and became suicidal. But, Taylor actually stole ideas from others to make himself successful, and was involved in making those despicable films. After this fact came out following his death at the hands of Cassandra Kimble, and together with Vernon's investigative and writing association with Vince Singleton which brought him on the road to self-empowerment, he and his wife started moving toward a reconciliation.

"I've felt like an outsider most of my life. You seem to have inherited my, ah, movie nerdy gene. I would spend my life alone, passively escaping into films, like

Woody Allen's character in *Play It Again, Sam.* Those made-up stories were so much more interesting than my dull and awkward way of dealing with the world, and just, I guess, reinforced my insecurities. I've learned that you have to be who you are, and be good with that. You'll find that your mother wouldn't want it any other way. Her love for you will transcend any prejudices that she harbors. You must give her a chance. She's done it with me, and she'll do the same for you."

Chapter Twenty-seven

10 AM Wednesday Morning

Vince Singleton's PTSD alertness had reached DEFCON 1. He was so on guard that he was getting whiplash from looking over his shoulders for possible threats in his surroundings. For a change he welcomed this session with Dr. Michael Probst. The psychologist's office felt like a safe retreat for a mind that felt under siege.

Vince had already told Probst about his increased symptoms, his lack of sleep and the nighttime patrols of the house looking for any vulnerabilities in his personal castle. He related nightmares that not only centered on Jewel's death, but on the other two women who were recently killed. However, his troubled dreams were not restricted to those victims. He told Probst of horrific visions where women were beaten, raped, and murdered in a hellish montage of violent images.

"It's awful, Doc. I haven't said anything to Hope or Gina. I don't want them to worry about me. But, I'm afraid to even doze off. I feel like I'm being haunted by all these crimes against women."

Probst did his usual eyeglass cleaning bit that usually indicated that he was ruminating over exactly how he was going to proceed.

"From what you said before, and the extent of these nightmares, it seems to me that you are still harboring a great deal of guilt. I want to stress that as long as we are not deliberately or recklessly endangering others, we all have to live our lives the best way we know how."

Probst stopped to take a drink of water but held up his hand to let Vince know that he wasn't finished and did not want to hear a rebuttal. Sometimes Vince wished Probst would step on the accelerator a bit with his insights.

"But there are a couple of details in these dreams that don't fit the deaths of Jewel, Lawrence and Josephs. I guess I'm trying to explore why you have become so involved in Cassandra's case, since the woman did try to kill you. Even though the abuse of women should be a shared concern of us all, your interest, I feel, is more personal. In your dreams, some of the assaults you envisioned took place, as you described, in a library or a bookstore. They seem like strange places for attacks to take place. Can you tell me why you think those locations show up in these nightmares?"

Vince did not want to look the psychologist straight on, so he stared out the large picture window at the Philadelphia skyline.

"I don't know," he said simply.

"Why do you think your mind placed these acts in places where there are books?"

"Just because I did,"

Probst offered a sly smile.

"That's what a child would say," said Probst. "Isn't that what Barbra Streisand's Dr. Lowenstein told Nick Nolte's Tom in *Prince of Tides*?"

Now it was Vince's turn to smile, letting Probst know that he appreciated the effort to relate to him by referencing a movie.

"I know why those settings show up in my dreams," said Vince. "I haven't told anyone this story, not Jewel, not even Hope or Gina, because I am ashamed about what I did, or more accurately what I didn't do."

Vince took a breath.

"There was this girl in college. Her name was Susan Foster. Very pretty, shapely, blonde hair. Dressed in a provocative style, you know, short, tight skirts and tops. She was in a couple of my English lit classes. I talked with her a bit, and even asked her out. She said I was nice, but she didn't see me that way. When you're older you realize some people are just not compatible romantically. But, being young, I was hurt. But that's not the real problem."

It was Vince's turn to take a drink of water to aid the flow of words.

"My parents didn't have much money. They were middle class. My dad had a clerical job with the Federal Government. My mom did some part-time secretarial work. I didn't feel deprived or anything like that. But, college tuition was expensive even back then for my family. So, when I heard there was some extra scholarship money the university was offering for undergraduates, I wanted to get my name in early with the Office of the Dean, who was coordinating the process. It was based on economic need and grades. My GPA was 3.95, so I figured I had a shot."

He started to feel hypocritical about blaming Probst for his slow-motion delivery.

"Anyway, I went to the Dean's office, knocked, but when I didn't get the 'come in' invite, I rudely tried opening the door. He should have locked it. I saw the Dean holding down Susan Foster on his desk, with his hand up her skirt and down her underwear. She was trying to push him off. When he saw me, he jumped away and Susan leaped off the desk and started to rearrange her clothes as she ran for the door. As we both were on our way out, the Dean warned us not to say anything or he would say we made up the whole thing to extort scholarship money from him, and we would be expelled."

Vince pulled a handkerchief out of his pocket and wiped briny sweat from his lip.

"I'd like to say that I told the Dean to go to hell. I'd like to tell you that I tried to comfort Susan. The fact is, I was embarrassed for all of us, and worried about my future. Later, when the memory of the assault forced its way into my consciousness, I would detour my mind into just focusing on the stacked bookcases in his office."

He stopped for a couple of seconds.

"She tried to talk to me shortly after the incident, but I avoided her and even rationalized my inaction by thinking at the time that Susan was at fault for dressing so seductively. What a crock. A woman could walk around naked, but it still does not justify anyone doing anything to harm her in any way. I let that jerk get away with it, and even worse, allowed him to maybe molest other young women."

Probst let out a slow sigh before speaking.

"I can see now why fighting against the abuse of women is so important to you. And, why you could feel that you may have precipitated these current crimes. But, I'll again appeal to your love of movies. In *Mississippi Burning*, would it have been better to allow the bigoted practices to continue because of a fear of retribution, or was it necessary to take a stand and suffer immediate hardship to gain future justice?"

Vince nodded his head. He knew the correct answer, but he did not feel like an unselfish do-gooder.

He had been guilty, like others, in allowing crimes against women to happen. He couldn't bear to be made a participant in any future attacks. There had to be a way to stop the violence.

Chapter Twenty-eight

8 PM Wednesday Evening

Samantha Hoffman loved watching Lt. Ray devour the veal piccata with angel hair pasta she had cooked up for them. He already used half a loaf of the crispy Tuscan bread to soak up the golden tangy butter and lemon sauce. He was a hungry man, hungry for food, information, and her. She rose from her seat across the dining room table and slowly moved her body wrapped in a tight, short dress over to where he sat. She liked the way material clung to her and she could see so did Ray. She squeezed herself between his chair and the plate of food and slid down onto his lap.

"Ready for something sweet?" she asked, and then not waiting for a reply to her rhetorical question kissed him hard.

Later in the roomy master bedroom of her new Lafayette Hill townhouse she reclined next to him, knowing the memory foam mattress would have a tough time bouncing back from the passionate indentations they had made together. The central air tried to cool them down. It was a strain on the system.

"Great dessert," said Newman. "And, it wasn't even fattening."

"Not that calories matter to you," she said as her arms gave him a squeeze. "Your metabolism burns right through everything."

"Well, your motor revs up pretty good, too," he said.

They both chuckled.

"I thought you could use a pleasurable way to blow off some steam. Your thermostat was reading in the red zone the other day at Vince's. Are you still carrying a mourning torch for Kate Lawrence?"

Newman shifted and untangled his body from Hoffman's. He propped himself on his right arm to look at her.

"No, that's not it. Sure, I had feelings for her once, and when you were close to someone it hurts more when something awful happens to that person. What's been gnawing at me is that Vince aligned himself with Cassandra Kimble. That kind of attachment invites trouble, and somebody answered that invitation."

Hoffman could see the faraway stare in Ray's eyes as they appeared to be looking in the distance for a solution to the dilemma posed by the situation. She raised herself on her left arm, looked at him with, she hoped, a soothing smile, and stroked his face with her right hand.

"Vince knows that Cassandra's warping started with men raping her from the time she was a child. He sees something in her worth saving. You may not agree that there is anything there to rescue, but try to consider that his cause is a just one that goes beyond just one woman."

Newman ran his left hand through his short brown buzz cut and then over his face.

"Vince left a voice message. He said that the group figured out that there were clues at both crime scenes that had to do with the film *Body Heat*."

"Well, that movie fits in well with *Basic Instinct*. Both have sexually liberated women who manipulate men and get away with their crimes," said Samantha.

She could see that the policeman in him was adrenalized.

"You know you want to get in on this, be a part of the hunt. You have to work it out with Vince. Right now, it's the only way to be in the game."

At that moment, Newman's cell phone rang. It was his father.

"Hey dad, how's it going."

"It's going, but slow," said Pete Newman. "Went through half the list of Jewel Singleton's patients. It's tough checking out to see if a connection to a cop exits. Of course, we're focusing on any ties to Patrick Campbell and Ned Edmunds, since they were the officers on site at Mrs. Singleton's shooting. I'll keep you posted if anything pans out."

"Thanks, dad. I appreciate it."

After he hung up she tied him up in her arms.

"For a guy on suspension, you're getting a lot of action tonight."

Chapter Twenty-nine

10 AM Thursday Morning

Lt. Harvey Douglas looked across his desk at Faye Patterson, but she did not look back. In fact, she surveyed the office, looking at his service citations on the wall behind him, the paperweight made of New Hampshire granite on his desk, even the hands in her lap which still wore her engagement and wedding rings. It didn't seem to Douglas that she was nervous. There were no agitated movements, no tightening of the facial muscles, no perspiration. She seemed relaxed, above it all, maybe even aloof, as if part of her mind wasn't even there. She had, in fact, tried to postpone the interview, and had pushed off the time of the meeting by an hour.

Douglas' team already completed some deep digging into the members of Vince Singleton's film class, and he ordered interviews zeroing in on those he felt deserved further delving. Because of her hostility toward Vince and what he described about her attitudes toward sexually liberated women, Douglas decided to talk with Mrs. Patterson himself. The lieutenant admired the thick layered fifty-five-year-old white hair with blonde highlights that did not have one strand out of place. Her black pullover top showed that she had not allowed gravity to pull her down or starchy foods to soften her up. She moved her right hand over her smooth gray skirt in an absent-minded gesture, just in case a wrinkle dared to put a crimp in her style.

She whipped her head around like a cannon mounted on its platform and pointed her now stern face at Douglas.

"Do I have to be here?" she said, which was more like an accusation than a question.

Douglas had to admit that she startled him.

"As you know, someone has murdered a member of your film class. We have reason to believe that it is the same person who killed the prominent female lawyer, Kate Lawrence. We are interviewing students who attended the class taught by Vince Singleton and Vernon Solomon. Did you know either Lawrence, or the other victim, Pauline Josephs?"

Since Mrs. Patterson did not respond quickly, Douglas leaned forward and said in a quiet voice, "It's just procedure to ask these questions. No one is accusing you of anything."

"Yet," she said, as if to finish the policeman's sentence. She resumed her Zen-like perusal of the room before she continued.

"The first time I saw the Josephs girl was at the class. I'm not surprised that her scantily clad costumes and her bordello makeup precipitated her demise. One cannot appear as she did without some type of consequences. From what I have read about the Lawrence woman's proclivities, I expect she caused the same reaction."

Douglas raised his eyebrows at the word "consequences," since it had appeared in one of the texts to Singleton. He tilted his head forward, as if to coax out the answer to his question. Faye Patterson noticed, and groaned.

"No, I did not know Kate Lawrence. Of course I knew of her. She was defending the indefensible seductress and killer, Cassandra Kimble."

Douglas waited for more, and when nothing followed, he pushed for a more revealing response.

"Yes, she represented the young lady who was involved romantically at one time with your husband before murdering him. Am I correct in saying that your hostility toward Ms. Kimble extended to her attorney?"

Mrs. Patterson produced a smirk of a smile that would not have won her the Miss Congeniality prize.

"The word 'lady' would never be the appropriate way to refer to that slutty, vicious Kimble girl. And, from what I have read about Lawrence, she was just an older depraved version of her client. Those two soiled the pristine reputations of upright women everywhere, who don't drain men of their virtue by opening them up to weakening temptation."

Douglas rubbed his hands together for a moment, looked down and softly chuckled quietly. The action elicited the attention from his guest that he desired. She looked at him with squinted eyes.

"I was not aware of saying anything funny, Lieutenant."

Douglas stopped smiling.

"I just find it interesting that you coincidentally enrolled in a class taught by a man who has supported the woman who was your husband's lover dash slayer. And, that two women, who you associate with the type of woman who killed Mr. Patterson, are now dead."

He paused for a second.

"But, that's not what amused me. It was that you took a course that presents a positive view of sexually liberated women in films."

It was Mrs. Patterson's turn to pause. She coupled the break with a throat clearing before speaking, but the aloofness was gone, and now Douglas felt she avoided eye contact to evade scrutiny.

"As I told Mr. Singleton, I was attending to expand my movie knowledge since I hope to perpetuate the legacy of the college film festival initiated by my dearly departed husband. Is there anything further?"

"Yes. I need to know where you were the nights of July 10th and 20th and were you with anyone at those times?"

It was the woman's turn to produce a short laugh.

"Like any decent, middle-aged widow, I was at my house, and I was alone. I have been reading a book that analyzes *film noir* movies for my now defunct class."

Douglas thought for a second.

"That book by any chance include anything on the films *Basic Instinct* and *Body Heat*?"

"Why, yes, unfortunately, those two movies fit into this unsavory genre."

Douglas stood up to signal the end of the interview. Mrs. Patterson followed his lead.

"Here is my card. Please contact me if you have anything else you may want to add to our conversation."

She took the card by securing it with the ends of her right thumb and index finger, holding it as if it contained some kind of infecting germ. She then nodded and turned to leave.

"I'll contact you if I need to question you further," said Douglas. "No need to give me any contact information. I've got your number. And, I know where you live."

Chapter Thirty

Friday Afternoon

Vince was again at the prison to talk with his favorite serial killer, looking for help in the strangest of places. He had already informed Cassandra about the clues at the last crime scene, and the references to *Body Heat*. She didn't have any insights concerning the Mace, and the DVD of *Hush ... Hush Sweet Charlotte*, or the dark stockings and short, tight skirt that were on Josephs' body.

"You have to admit it is odd that you keep visiting the person who tried to ghost you," said Cassandra.

"Relatives and friends would agree with your observation," said Vince. "Maybe I have developed a death wish."

Cassandra shook her long black hair.

"Sorry, can't accommodate you. I've sworn off. But I do like talking about the zany antics of other predators. Any forensic evidence who wish to share?"

Vince shook his head.

"Nada. Douglas called me and said there weren't any prints or DNA evidence that shouldn't be at the victims' two homes. Looks like you 21st century felons are learning to dodge the forensic bullet."

Cassandra folded her arms in front of her and stretched her legs as she sat across from him while several guards fitted with nightsticks and Tasers stood close by.

"Yeah, some of us stay ahead of the curve. But, now I am just a boring writer. Is there any fun in your humdrum legit life, Vince?"

He laughed.

"I wish my life could be dull for a change. But, for some reason you people keep wanting me to play *Catch Me if You Can* with movie clues, and if I don't figure things out, bodies drop. And, I get hounded by the press, I get tons of annoying emails ..."

"Kvetch, kvetch, kvetch," said Cassandra, in a Southern drawl.

"Okay, Norma Rae, I'll stop complaining," chuckled Vince.

"And, watch that 'you people' stuff. Makes you sound like a bigot."

After a couple of chuckles, Cassandra became serious.

"Have you come across anybody who fits the pattern? Anybody who looks like an abuser?"

Vince thought for a minute, and then shook his head.

"No, not really. You know that it's difficult to see outward signs. They can turn it off and on very easily."

"Anybody with low self-esteem?" asked Cassandra.

"Well, there is this one student, Joe Goldman. He seems unsure of himself, fumbles in his speech, and looks to me for validation. He's been following my film blog and posted several comments. But, that, in and of itself, doesn't mean anything."

Cassandra's eyes seemed to be staring off into the distance, as if she were looking beyond the walls around them, transporting herself to another place, or time, before speaking again.

"Any objectification of women, disrespecting them?"

Vince considered whether he should say anything that might agitate Cassandra. He personally knew how current events could act as stressors which regurgitated past trauma. She had done some heavy psychological lifting to reconstruct her damaged life, and he didn't want to undermine the work she was doing. But, they had built trust between them, so he wanted to be honest.

"These two class members, young guys, Ike Lacy and Bill Herrman made sexual comments as Pauline Josephs walked away at the last session. And, Lacy had been in a previous class with her, and tagged her as a heartbreaker."

Cassandra raised her hands up as if to indicate a revelation was at hand.

"In and of itself, that doesn't indicate anything," said Vince. "Males comment on the way women look and act all the time. Yes, they were being inappropriate and unfortunately men still do objectify women, but they don't all become killers."

"There might be less violence against women if men wouldn't just give priority to their ding-dongs," said Cassandra. "Did you notice anybody being a control freak, power-hungry, jealous ..."

"Isolated, hypersensitive, ill-tempered. I know the what-to-look-out-for list. I don't know of any abusers in my personal life, and I haven't become very acquainted with the people in my professional world. Social butterflying, as you know, is not my thing. But, this murderer could be anybody, not necessarily someone I have met. It could be someone who's heard about me in the news."

Cassandra raised her eyebrows and nodded as if to show she would like to agree. She hesitated before

148

speaking again, copying Vince's beat-taking, almost appearing to not want to proceed.

"Yeah, Mr. S., but I wanted to be able to be part of the action, witness your responses, be in the game. And, since our new kid on the block is sort of opposite copy-catting me by using movie clues to take out women, he may want to be … involved, too."

She paused, as if wanting to move away from reminding Vince that the killer may be close by.

"I know I said 'he.' But, I can be objective. Maybe it's a female. How about Mrs. Tight-Ass Patterson. She's plenty pissed at me, and could have been angry at my lawyer, and probably considers you to be a traitor, playing nice with me. If she did it, and you catch her, you can then visit her, too."

Vince grunted and said, "No way. She's no fun to talk with. Unlike you."

Cassandra said, "Aw," and gave herself a hug and batted her eyelids in an exaggerated thank-you.

"Oh, the producer who will be working on the movie version of my book agreed to take a look at your screenplay, and said he'd get back to me shortly," said Vince.

"Fingers-crossed!" said a smiling Cassandra while overlapping her digits.

Chapter Thirty-one

Saturday Morning

Brunch after bullets. Gina Alimentare never thought those two "b's" would buzz one after the other in her life. The food for sure, being an Italian American from South Philly. Well, the ammo was also there in her former neighborhood, first with the old Mafia types and now with inner city violence. It was sad, but she didn't know anybody who had stayed where she grew up, not even her parents. She hardly even visited her old neighborhood in South Philly anymore, except to visit Cavatello's Bakery to buy some amazing almond cookies, rum cake, and cannoli. After her divorce from her husband, who could have been the poster boy for arrested development, and leaving her home in that neighborhood for an apartment on Lombard Street near the center part of Philadelphia, she felt like a foreigner now whenever she visited the area where she grew up.

Even with what had happened with Vince and Cassandra, she never thought about using a firearm. The damn things scared her. But, now, with another threat of violence, possibly aimed at women in Vince's life, she had to reconsider. After all, the police can't be everywhere. She still believed in background checks and limiting automatic weapons. Also, she thought, if you had to take a test to drive a car, why shouldn't there be classes, tests, and licensing to use a device meant for destruction?

Samantha Hoffman showed her how to load, unload, aim, stand, and squeeze the trigger. She was a good student, enough so that Samantha had called her a "natural" with a pistol. But, there was something that worried her after her time earlier at the firing range. She looked across at her eating companion as the biology professor attacked her Eggs Benedict.

"What? Do I have yoke on my face?" asked Samantha as she saw Gina staring at her.

"I sort of liked it," said Gina in a low voice as if not wanting anyone to hear her confession. "I mean, I feel awful about it, but, shooting the gun gave me a thrill. What does that say about me?"

"That you're no different than many other people," said Samantha with a smile. "It also feels a lot safer when it's just target practice. It's a protected way to experience the power there, and it can be exhilarating for women, who have been denied empowerment."

After years of growing up in the South Philly male-dominated Italian culture, power was something Gina was not used to, although she knew she left her husband and the place of her youth because she needed to develop her own strength. She considered Samantha's words for a moment. But she still felt uneasy.

"Something exhilarating can become addictive."

"That's when you have to also have strength, to know when not to pull the trigger," said Samantha, as she slid a small shopping bag under the table to Gina.

"I have two guns. I'm lending you my Smith and Wesson .32 caliber. If it was good enough for Cassandra, it's good enough for us."

Gina shook her head and started to push away from the table.

"Take it," said Samantha. "You don't have the luxury to consider your principles right now. This killer isn't giving you the time for that."

***

Patrick Campbell sat in his dark blue Dodge Charger, inhaling and exhaling the smoke coming from his cigar, his nose taking in the biting odor of the tobacco's exhaust. He stroked the rough texture of the leather-covered steering wheel, thinking how he liked muscle in his car. No wimpy hybrid for him. He followed Pete Newman to his son's apartment after Smartley had told him that he should check out the retired cop after he discovered he was getting inside information from his old partner, Fred Danson. Campbell was starting to think that the father was becoming as much of a pain-in-the-ass as his son. *Bad genes*, he thought. To Campbell, these guys were worse than the criminals they said they were out to get. They were traitors to their own kind. And he knew what kind of punishment traitors deserved.

***

Newman looked at his father with a smile, and Pete Newman, looking up from the copied paperwork that he had placed on the coffee table in his son's apartment, almost seemed irritated at the appearance on his son's face.

"What the hell are you grinning at? You makin' fun of me? You've been a lieutenant, for, like how long? A lunch break?"

Newman maintained his jovial look as he waved his hands in front of him as if to fend off the misinterpreted attack.

"At ease, officer. You got me all wrong. You came in here revved up, talking fast. I'm just glad to see you feeling good about being on the job again."

Pete relaxed his shoulders which had squared off and looked as if they belonged to a fullback ready to bang through a defensive line. He seemed a bit embarrassed about his enthusiasm, and looked at the coffee table as he spoke.

"Yeah, well, I always liked it when I could get to the bottom of something when I was on the force. It was the investigative part of the work that I got a kick out of. Not the banging down doors and cuffing people. Anyway, here's what I came up with."

He started handing his son police records.

"My pal Fred Danson made these copies on the Q.T. He got a hit on a young black woman by the name of Linda York from the list of Jewel Singleton's clients. Police records show that she was a CI several years ago for Detective Patrick Campbell. She apparently was involved with a guy who had a gang that did some burglaries. He used her to deal dope, and she was caught. Was probably looking for protection when Campbell keyed in on her. Could be something there, right?"

Newman nodded his head and said, "Yeah, maybe, maybe. We got some info where we can find her?"

Pete made a face that the younger Newman had seen before when his father had hit a wall when working on a case. His right cheek tightened, puffing up that side of his face, which made his mouth crooked and squinted his right eye.

"That's the problem. She's dead. Killed. Knifed. That boyfriend is doing time for the crime. Records show he says he didn't do it, but the weapon was found in his possession."

"Damn," said Newman. He rubbed his face with his right hand and looked at the wall as if trying to read on it what to do next.

"What about relatives? Maybe we can find out something there," he said.

"Thought about that, too," said Pete. "She has a sister. A Barbara Barancik. Divorced. Has a daughter. She was living in an apartment in Germantown at the time of her sister's death. I did some research and she is still in that part of the city, but now rents a house."

Newman smiled again.

"Good work, Pop."

Pete did the tight right cheek thing again.

"I tried calling her. But, she was a bit hostile. Wanted to know who the hell I was, asking questions. I told her, and she said she didn't have anything to say to anyone, especially some badge-less ex-cop."

"Well, there is a problem there," said Newman. "You have no clout, and neither do I at this point. Plus, she probably blames the police for causing that boyfriend to get amped up, going after his snitch of a girlfriend."

Newman closed his eyes for a couple of seconds, then popped them open.

"She may, however, be more inclined to talk to a news reporter."

Chapter Thirty-two

Saturday Evening

Vince was sautéing mushrooms and had just added some tomatoes, carrots, and broccoli while Gina checked the boiling penne so they would not become too soft. His sensitive digestive system steered him into making pasta primavera because acidic tomato sauce many times lit up his heartburn problem. He liked serving the dish with ricotta on the side and grated Parmesan cheese sprinkled over the pasta. For Gina's sake, he usually placed black pepper on the dinner table.

As he stirred the vegetable ingredients around with a spatula, there was a knock at the family room door. Hope, who had been reading the screenplay of *Crash* as Jellybean snoozed next to her, went to the door, looked through the peephole, smiled, and opened it. Newman was standing there, with a bag which had the Wegmans supermarket name on it.

"Oooh, what ya' got there?" asked Hope.

"It's a bag of assorted cookies. Got some chocolate chip, macadamia nut, peanut butter, and just for a token attempt at being healthy, a few oatmeal raisin. I know your dad is the Cookie Monster of his street."

"Come on in," said Hope. "We were just getting dinner together. You know you're welcome to stay, especially now that you brought dessert."

As Newman walked into the house, Vince knew that Hope was again playing the role of diplomat as she often had done when he and Jake had their brotherly battles.

"Hi, Lieutenant," said Vince.

"Yeah, hi," said Newman.

There was an uncomfortable silence. Vince realized that it took a lot of effort for Newman to come knocking with his conciliatory confections, and the least Vince could do was respond in culinary kind.

"Yeah, we're making a Clemenza amount of pasta here. Why don't you join us?"

Newman seemed relieved as he smiled and let out a sigh.

"When have you known me to ever turn down food?"

They all sat at the dinner table in the area just beyond the kitchen and which was at a right angle to the living room. While they ate, they avoided talking about the killings until Gina brought up the target practice.

"Tell Samantha thanks again for her help today. I appreciate her looking out for my safety."

Vince shifted in his chair and looked at his plate with a smile-deprived face. Newman noticed.

"You know, a lot of cops are not too thrilled with amateurs using firearms," the lieutenant said. "We are concerned about innocent people, and police officers, getting caught in the well-meaning, but inexperienced crossfire."

Vince nodded his head in exaggerated agreement.

"I'm with you on that. I think the less guns, the better."

"You believe in self-defense, or else you wouldn't be practicing throwing those knives of yours around," said Gina.

Vince shook his head.

"It's different. You can't cause the kind of destruction with knives that bullets can inflict. And, you don't accidentally throw a knife at someone, while there are accidental shooting deaths all of the time."

"The police worry most about the violence of street gangs, and their fighting over their drug-dealing turfs," said Newman. "But, it's difficult to crack down on illegal firearms."

"At least we should clamp down on the legal sale of weapons," said Vince. "Can't we have laws that make classes in the proper use of guns mandatory? And, if we had background checks on everybody who bought firearms, even at gun shows, we could eliminate some of the psychos from getting them. And, should there really be sales of automatic assault weapons and high capacity magazines? Pretty soon, these weapon enthusiasts are going to say it's okay to have your own Howitzer!"

He realized that Gina knew he was upset by the ghosts of the deaths that haunted his waking and sleeping dreams, so she had allowed him his rant before speaking.

"What you say makes a great deal of sense when you're analyzing the problem objectively. But, things aren't so clear-cut when there's a killer out there who is targeting people you actually know, and maybe ones that you truly care about. Let's face it, with no disrespect to the police, they have too much on their plates."

Newman shrugged his shoulders.

"Unofficially, I have to agree with Gina. And, the way I like to chow down, I always have too much on my plate."

Before Vince could continue to try to disarm his dinner companions, Hope spoke up.

"I know one thing we can all agree on loading up on – those cookies that Lt. Ray brought us. I'll make the coffee."

They all smiled, helped gather up the empty dinner plates, and put the leftover food into the refrigerator. They sat down in the family room and enjoyed their coffee and dessert. Vince could see that Newman needed to get something off his food-extended chest.

"So, what's on your mind, Ray?"

Newman wiped his face with a napkin and rose from his chair. He walked over to a bookcase near the outside doorway and leaned against it.

"I just wanted to say that I was wrong. It's not your fault what's happened. You can't be responsible for what damaged people think and how they act. Look, I still am not sure that your dealings with Cassandra Kimble are a good idea. But, I realize that you are fighting for a principle here, and it's hard not to support you on your efforts to motivate people against violence against women."

Vince gave out a relieved sigh, glad that the tension between him and Newman was dissipating.

"Thanks. But, trust me, I struggle with guilt every day. Many times I think I should have never written a word about Cassandra and, after she was imprisoned, it would have been better if I would have sealed myself off in my own solitary confinement."

"Well, before you incarcerate yourself, let's try to work together to catch some bad guys," said Newman, and he proceeded to tell what his father had learned, and suggested using Jake to do some digging.

Vince considered what he heard.

"Well, although I hate to admit it, it worked before. Guess I better give my brother a call."

Chapter Thirty-three

Sunday Morning

Vince was still groggy from another half-slept night filled with nightmares and anxiety when his cell phone, sitting on the snack table next to his cup of decaf coffee, started to buzz. Gina and Hope were sitting on the couch next to his lounger as they watched CBS Sunday Morning when the sound interrupted their concentration, causing them to whip their heads in synchronized movement toward the sound.

Vince looked at them and saw apprehension in their eyes, which he was sure was what they saw in his. He sucked in a deep breath, picked up the device, entered his four-digit access code, and read the text message. He exhaled a sigh that he knew the other two thought was one of relief. They were only half right.

"Not our homicidal friend?" asked Gina with a smile.

"Oh, it's the killer, alright," said Vince.

"Holy Havarti, why are you looking so calm?" yelled Hope.

Vince gave his daughter a crooked look.

"What is it with you and the religious food combos?"

Hope just shrugged.

"I'm not as alarmed as I could be because the message isn't saying that there is another victim that I should be asking the police about. Here is what it says:

'My name is not Clarice, so silence is not what I seek, Vince. When are you talking to me again? If not soon, another one of your women may be erased from existence. The clues were there. Have you found any more of them? Obviously not enough to save poor Pauline.'"

Vince looked at Hope and nodded. She realized he wanted her to translate for Gina.

"The reference to Clarice ..."

"I got that one," said Gina. "Hannibal Lecter. *Silence of the Lambs*."

"Right," said Hope. "I don't see any significance to the line other than he is showing that he is the killer, and in charge."

"Yeah, I agree," said Vince. "Clarice is the FBI agent trying to find out what's going on. Our murderer here already knows, and I think he is implying that I am Clarice in this scenario."

Gina knitted her eyebrows together in thought before saying what thoughts she wove together.

"I think it's interesting that you are cast as a woman. I think it goes to our predator's mindset of being dominant over his female prey."

Vince shook his head in approval.

"Not bad, as long as the killer is a man. Otherwise, it is an attempt to lead me to that assumption," he said. He looked again at Hope to continue her explication.

"That 'erased from existence' line is, like, definitely from *Back to the Future*. It's what the Doc says is going to happen to Marty if he doesn't straighten out the past."

It was Vince's turn to be pensive for a bit before speaking. When he spoke, he knew his voice was shaky because his guilt was rattling him.

"I think I am being told to look at the clues that are now part of the past, so I can fix the future. If I had been successful in figuring them out, Pauline Josephs might still be alive."

Hope came over to his chair and gripped his shoulders as if trying to steady her father.

"You have been put in a terrible position, here, Dad. As you have always told me, we can't change the past, so there's no use dwelling on what we could have done. We have to focus on what we have to do now."

Vince looked up at Hope and patted one of her hands with his as he wiped a tear away with his other.

"You better answer the text," said Gina. "Show that you're still playing along."

Vince nodded and sent a text stating how the latest set of clues referred to *Body Heat*, and that the pajamas at the first crime scene referred to Pauline Josephs. He received a reply text right after he finished. Vince read it:

"Good work, Vince. If you hadn't participated, I may have had to erase someone ahead of schedule to get you back on the playing field. But, the clock is ticking. Better up your game."

The threat sunk in until Vince could feel it lay like a brick in his gut.

"I guess I better touch base with Douglas. He'll want to check my cell again. For all the good it will do."

Chapter Thirty-four

Monday Morning

Despite the early time of day, Lt. Douglas was already in third gear as he ploughed through the information on his laptop that the detectives provided him. He still had to sift through heaps of details to separate the pertinent from the irrelevant. He already reviewed the entries on the film class member in front of him, Bill Herrman.

"Nice piece of hardware you have there," said the young man.

Douglas did not appreciate Herrman trying to direct the conversation. His response was not accompanied by a smile.

"It gets me through the day."

He decided to pick up on the topic, though.

"IT fellow, right? Know how to find out about things, people? I just know to type and click. But, you, you must know all about computers, cell phones, texting, how to protect privacy, how to hack?"

Herrman rubbed his palms on the legs of his pants and looked straight at Douglas.

"Yeah, I know about protecting systems *against* hacking."

Douglas looked back at his laptop and spoke while looking at the screen."

"By the way, thank you for coming in today for this interview."

Herrman smiled and said, "Didn't really have a choice, did I?"

Douglas looked at him and smiled as he spoke.

"Why did you get into the tech field?"

Herrman shrugged.

"It's what's trending. Besides, I seem to have a knack for it," he said as he pushed the large frame of his eyeglasses up the bridge of his nose in a classic nerd move.

"And why the interest in movies?" asked Douglas.

Herrman removed his hands from his legs and sort of just threw them up into the air.

"I don't know. I guess it's a nice change of pace, looking at stories on a screen instead of steps in an algorithm. I always liked watching films when I was a kid."

It was Douglas' turn to toss up a hand.

"Any favorite types of flicks you like more than others."

Herrman wasn't on pause for long.

"Well here's where the logic in science and in the plans of the filmmakers comes together. See, I like solving computer mysteries. And in really good movies, say like those made by Alfred Hitchcock, there are so many parts to the psychological puzzles that I get a rush analyzing how they all come together."

Douglas nodded his head.

"Okay. You like mysteries. Maybe you can help me with this one. How come an intelligent, seemingly unthreatening young man would be charged with cyber bullying a young woman?"

Herrman looked like he turned to stone.

"See, it says here on my screen that you had a restraining order against you, and were sued for libel?"

Herrman closed his eyes, inhaled deeply and then exhaled slowly until it seemed to Douglas that he not only expelled the air but also the anger that would have erupted if allowed to build up.

"Does it also say there that the libel suit was dismissed because the fact that I called her a sleazy seductive whore-thief could not be disproved? Does it tell you that she met me at an IT conference, threw herself at me, promised that we would be partners in love and business, and then stole an app I developed to easily and swiftly provide online access to every conceivable type of information about films? Does it also inform you that I am in the process of suing her for intellectual property theft?"

Douglas economically gave a one-nod head response.

"Oh, yeah, I have that here, too. I mean, at least about both of your legal actions," he said. "But, you used stronger, derogatory language about her online than what you just said. And, that restraining order came about after you went to her place of work and threw, let me see here, your Google Chromebook at her."

"It was hers, not mine. I may have been angry, but I'm not stupid. She should have all her files deleted, if you know what I mean."

Douglas cocked his head.

"You get pretty steamed up when you're not doing your little yoga breathing exercise there, don't you?"

Herrman did the eyeglass push-up again.

"Even a peaceful man can have his limits tested," he said.

Douglas closed the laptop.

"Guess it's my job to go after the person that fails that test."

Chapter Thirty-five

Tuesday, Early Evening

As Jake Newman drove along Wissahickon Avenue in the Germantown section of Philadelphia, he passed the Department of Veterans Affairs Regional Office and Insurance Center. His post-traumatic stress disorder produced flashbacks of his duty in Vietnam, but the prolonged process of filing his disability claim with the government agency also gave him recurring nightmares. To be fair, the government was just starting to wrestle with the diagnosis during the period following the Southeast Asia conflict. In the past, the mental condition was called, rather negatively, "shell shock," and it was thought of as a disease restricted to cowards. But with persistence, the help of the Disabled American Veterans, and a letter to his congressman, Jake won his appeal for benefits.

Further study into the nature of PTSD showed that it occurred in individuals exposed to all sorts of traumatic events, such as the one his brother experienced when he lost Jewel. Jake thought about his sister-in-law, as he often did, and marveled at how nonjudgmental and caring she was. And what a great sense of humor. He remembered that silly joke she told about the 95-year-old man who complained to his doctor that he couldn't pee anymore, and the physician said, "Well, you've peed enough." Jake chuckled to himself, but then thought about the sister of Linda

York, and what dark dreams she must have about her murdered sibling.

The rap sheet on Linda that Newman's father acquired noted several arrests for possession of illegal drugs, mostly cocaine. But what he needed to find out was if there was any connection between her death and that of Jewel's. He was hoping to get help finding that link from her sister, Barbara Barancik. Jake had called her, but it was not easy persuading her to meet him. She sounded paranoid, as if whatever danger that destroyed her sister could somehow enshroud her, too. He convinced Barbara by asking her to look him up on the Internet, and promised that he was trying to find out who was responsible for Linda's death. Barbara said she could only see Jake in between her day job as a dental technician and her cashier gig in the evening at Lowe's. He turned onto Greene Street, and parked a few doors down from her house. Barbara must have been watching through her window because Jake didn't even have to knock before the faded brown door swung open.

"So, you that reporter, huh?" said Barbara.

Jake gave her that ear-to-ear Dennis Quaid smile.

"Yes, mam. That I am."

"Singleton, right?"

"Just call me Jake."

"Well, come on in then. My mama told me it ain't proper to have a conversation with someone in the doorway."

Jake followed Barbara into the living room which had a sofa and chair with matching floral upholstery. Seated in the chair with one leg draped over the armrest and a book open in her lap was a young girl, probably around twelve years old.

"This here is my daughter, Sharleen. Girl, say hello to the man."

Sharleen looked up with a sly smile.

"Hello, man," she said.

"Don't you start with that smart mouth," said Barbara. "Now go upstairs and do your homework there. The adults have some talkin' to do."

Sharleen raised herself up in slow motion, as if the chair she was seated in had an increased gravitational pull. She gathered up her books and laptop and ascended the stairs with a loud sigh. Barbara watched her daughter climb to the next floor and when she heard the door to the bedroom close, she spoke.

"That girl is smart, probably smarter than I am, and I'm smart. She is a bit lazy, though, but I'll cure her of that. She likes science. Gonna' go to college. Maybe become a doctor."

Barbara went to the kitchen and brought out some cold lemonade which Jake gratefully accepted on this hot day. He sat down in the now vacant chair, and, after gulping down the pleasantly sweet liquid, he was ready to get to work.

"I don't know much about your sister, Linda. Maybe you can fill me in on what she was like, and what you think happened to her."

Barbara put her half-full glass of lemonade onto an end table next to the sofa.

"Jake, tell me why you're so interested in my sister, when everybody else seems to have forgotten about her."

Jake had only mentioned on the phone that he had come across the story of Linda York's death while investigating another killing, and was exploring the possibility of the two being related. He now told her about Jewel's death, and the involvement in that incident with Detective Patrick Campbell. Barbara clenched her jaw and squinted her eyes when he mentioned the policeman.

"Didn't like that man. He used my sister when she was on the outs. You have to understand something about Linda. She was a good young woman until the drugs got a hold of her. She did her homework, worked chores around the house, did babysitting to earn some money. But then life added a 'dys' to our functional family."

Barbara looked at her lemonade with a quizzical expression, as if trying to find something in the glass that would explain why things went wrong. She drank some more of the cold drink before continuing.

"Our father was a hardworking man. An electrician, a good trade, and he provided for our family. Linda and him went together like hominy and grits. Those two would tell each other bad jokes and still laugh like hyenas. Dad liked that Linda always asked questions about his tools. When the four of us would watch TV, those two would talk back to the characters on the sitcoms. Used to piss me and mother off something terrible while they was doing it, but then we would all laugh together in the end."

She smiled and just shook her head as she remembered. Then the smile vanished.

"But things changed, as they do. Papa while going to a job was killed by a hit-and-run driver. Cops never did find out who the reckless, cowardly bastard was. Mama, well she just fell to pieces. Wouldn't eat, stayed in bed. Tried to kill herself once with sleeping pills. Me and Linda found her on the bedroom floor, called 911, saved her. But for what? She's still in the mental hospital."

Jake felt like he had to say something, but sometimes even writers don't have the words.

"I'm so sorry," was all he could manage. "So I'm guessing all of this sadness must have led to Linda's drug use."

Barbara nodded her head.

"She was going to Temple University, working toward being an elementary school teacher, when this hard time visited us. I had my girl who was a baby at the time, and even though my marriage went bad, my Sharleen kept me going. But Linda, she missed her father so much, and after what happened to mother, well, Linda, she just looked for a way to deal. It was the wrong way, of course. She dropped out of school after she started with the crack. Then, to make money, she started to sell drugs. That's when she got busted."

Jake drained the rest of his lemonade.

"And that's when she became involved with Campbell, made a deal to escape prosecution, I'm guessing, and became his confidential informant."

Barbara gave a sad chuckle.

"Oh, she was more than that. He wormed his way into her life. He seemed to know where she was all the time, showed up wherever she may be. He bought her stuff. Clothes, jewelry, and such. She let him have his way with her, but his way was rough. She wanted out, but once you're under the thumb of a bad policeman, you got no place to go. Especially if you're a young girl who is a drug dealer. Nobody is going to believe that you're the victim. They only see you as a criminal."

Jake checked his notes.

"A boyfriend, Leon Clayton, was tried and convicted of second degree murder. Do you think he killed Linda?"

Barbara shook her head vigorously.

"No, sir, I do not. Now, Leon was no prize, nowhere near. He was a thief, and had my sister dealing drugs. But, he cared about her, although that caring took place in his world of crime. The cops said Leon was arrested for robbing houses and killed Linda while waiting for his trial because he thought that Linda ratted him out. It wasn't her! It was probably a rival gang member who spilled. No, I think it was that dirty cop Campbell that ended my Linda."

Barbara was shaking now, and wrapped her arms around her upper body to steady herself.

"But, what was I supposed to do? I had no evidence. The knife belonged to Leon, but he said that it was taken from his place and used to frame him. His crooked word didn't mean anything. This is how it goes."

Jake needed something more, something or someone who could implicate Campbell.

"Did your sister give you anything written, or send you texts or emails talking about how she felt threatened by Detective Campbell."

Barbara shook her head.

"No, she was worried he would find out. She was very paranoid, and that shit can be catchy, because I started looking over my shoulder, too. That Campbell came sniffing around here before Leon was charged, pretending like he was trying to find her killer. He asked if there was anything my sister gave me for safe-keeping that might contain clues to her death. I let him search the place so he would leave me alone. I just wanted that man gone."

"Did you know that your sister was seeking psychological counseling from Jewel Singleton?"

"No. But I'm glad she was trying to get help. Just makes it sadder that she couldn't get a chance to use it."

Jake was feeling frustrated, but there was still one more possibility.

"Okay, Linda may have kept certain things from you, to protect you, because it would be easy for her killer to find family members. But, maybe there was someone else she might confide in, a friend maybe?"

Barbara sat back on the sofa and rubbed her chin for a few moments before removing her hand and raising her index finger.

"There was a young lady she became friends with at college. They stayed close after she left. She would try to get Linda to go to those meetings for addicted people after my sister left school. I met her a few times. Nice girl. Her name is Nancy Dahl."

Jake rose from his chair.

"You wouldn't happen to know how I could get in touch with her, would you?"

Barbara smiled.

"I do believe I have her phone number."

Chapter Thirty-six

Wednesday Afternoon

Vince looked at the dishes of food in front of him and wondered if he would survive the culinary test. He decided he would not go down to defeat without a fight, so he grasped the knife and fork and attacked with his weapons of digestion. The brisket at David's Deli on Montgomery Avenue near Narberth, Pennsylvania, was lean and tender, and the mashed potatoes were smooth and buttery. Gina almost growled when she bit into her Reuben sandwich which was accompanied by her favorite dish there, the outwardly crisp and inwardly fluffy potato pancakes. One thought of tennis balls given the size of the matzos floating in the large bowl of chicken flavored soup in front of Hope. Mark decided on breakfast food, which consisted of eight large slices of syrupy drenched Challah French toast.

After several mouthfuls of food, Hope addressed Vince.

"Bill Herrman, you know, from the film class, texted me. He said it would be really cool if some of us could, like, get together, and continue to discuss the themes and relevant movies that were on the syllabus. I mean, we could just meet ourselves, but if you want to join in, that would be cool."

Vince exchanged a dramatic look with Gina, and then finished chewing what was in his mouth. Before he could say anything, Hope, probably guessing that there was some meaning in the looks between the two, spoke up.

"Okay, what gives? There you go, not telling me things again."

"Michael Caine's line to his boss, Ross, in *The Ipcress File*," said Mark in between bites of his French toast.

"Of course, we're doing the movie quotes thing again," said Gina with what sounded to Vince like a resigned tone. Vince wiped his mouth, and then spoke.

"I talked with Lt. Douglas. He and his crew have investigated some members of the class. Turns out Herrman had anger issues with a certain female."

Vince went on to inform Hope and Mark about Herrman's online attacks, and the restraining order and libel lawsuit against him.

"I knew there was something wrong about that guy," said a heated Mark. He addressed Hope. "You told him about us, but he kept texting you. You said he was a sweet, intelligent dude. Looks like he's nasty underneath."

It was Hope's turn to burn a bit, which was against her arbitrating nature.

"Didn't you stop to listen to the whole story? He was getting ripped off by that chick. You're not the only one who has righteous rage, you know."

Vince knew Mark was an angry young man himself. The hurt from the early death of his father still pained the young man. Plus, the practice of using animals in laboratory experiments to test medical treatments that didn't pan out, and causing them to suffer fueled Mark's anger, which spilled over into other areas.

"Okay, you two. Let's calm down. Maybe we can work something out here," said Vince.

He thought for several seconds before talking again.

"Maybe we can use this opening by Herrman. He has shown hostility toward a woman who seduced him. Ike Lacy admitted to knowing Pauline Josephs in the past. Joe Goldman has some kind of fan fixation with me, so he might have a motive to try to impress me with his movie mojo. And, Faye Patterson sees me as a traitor to her husband's memory. Maybe it would be a good idea to observe them, and others from the class, at an unofficial gathering of the members."

Gina seemed upset.

"You and Hope should have some protection at this kind of meeting. Suppose the killer is one of the class members?

"We can't have obvious police types there. It would put the perpetrator on guard," countered Vince.

"Yeah, but you can have others there that you know," said Mark. "I'm definitely going to be part of this thing. I want to keep an eye on Herrman. And we should ask James and Evan to be there, too, along with his dad."

"Sounds like a good idea to me," said Vince. "Let's get the word out to meet tomorrow evening, Thursday, the night we were holding the class."

Vince could see the apprehension in Gina's eyes.

"We're going to a public site. Let's announce that we're holding the get-together at The Bean Counter coffee house on Lancaster Avenue at 7 pm."

Chapter Thirty-seven

Thursday Evening

Vince thought that The Bean Counter served the best decaf white chocolate mocha in the Philadelphia area. Maybe one could argue that point, but there was no denying they poured it to the brim of the largest mug of any coffee house. No contest there. Gina ordered her usual hazelnut latte with whipped cream. Hope opted for the iced salted caramel mocha. The smells coming from their cups intermingled with those of the other patrons, and the combined aromas acted as a soothing incense, calming Vince's agitated mind.

They arrived early, but Vernon Solomon and his son, Evan, were already seated at a large table in the back room. Just as they finished exchanging their hello's, Mark Goodner and James Player walked in. Ike Lacy and Joe Goldman showed up minutes apart, followed by Bill Herrman, who produced a large smile in response to Hope's greeting, which was followed by a scowl on Mark's face. Vince was again surprised to see Faye Patterson come into the room. She sat down after ordering a cup of chamomile tea without looking at the others seated at the table. After taking a few sips, she raised her head and noticed Vince staring at her.

"What? I told you that I needed the film background for the festival. Since the class was canceled I wasn't going to waste an opportunity to sit in on another session. I'm not thrilled with the topic of the course, but it does cover a number of movies," she said, and went right back to drinking her tea in silence.

The three other classmates who regularly participated in the two sessions, the middle-aged Jeffrey Shestack, and the younger Jennifer Walsh and Debra Pearl, appeared with mugs of coffee and sat down at the table. It was 7:10 pm, so Vince decided to get the meeting going.

"A few of you wished to continue gathering informally to further explore the class material that both Dr. Solomon and I introduced in our first two sessions. I'm surprised but gratified that others showed up here tonight, given the circumstances surrounding the fate of one of the students, Pauline Josephs. I know that what happened to her was very disturbing, and that you have been, or will, be contacted by the police to help in any way with the investigation."

"It looks like, at least from news that's been trending, that her death was linked to the murder of that attorney, Kate Lawrence. Are you involved with both investigations, Mr. Singleton?" asked a bug-eyed Joe Goldman.

Vince paused for a moment to consider his response.

"First off, given the informal nature of our session here, please call me Vince."

Goldman seemed very pleased, a grin radiating from his face, probably because Vince said to call him by his first name.

"And to answer your question, Joe, yes, I am. But I am not at liberty to discuss anything about that topic. Let's stick with the movies, because that is why we are really here. There are a few people here who were former students of mine. That's Mark Goodner, James

Player, and Dr. Solomon's son, Evan. Professor Gina Alimentare teaches at PSCU."

There were no other comments, so Vince decided to begin the discussion.

"I'm sorry I can't show scenes from the films we will discuss, but we listed them in the syllabus, so I am hoping you saw them recently, or did so in the past. I'll begin by asking with what film was Roman Polanski modeling his noir classic, *Chinatown*, after?"

"Dah," said James as soon as the words were out of Vince's mouth, "an easy $200 question on Jeopardy – What is *The Maltese Falcon*?"

"Right you are, James. Yes, Faye Dunaway's character in *Chinatown* is built on the femme fatale classical base, which includes Mary Astor's role in *The Maltese Falcon*. Dunaway's Mrs. Mulwray appears vulnerable, thus seducing the male for her purposes, but she hides secrets."

"That's for sure," emphasized Ike Lacy. "She was in an incestual relationship with her own father. How filthy is that?"

"That's why her girl is her daughter, her sister, I mean her daughter," said Jeffrey Shestack in a mocking attempt to mimic the character's dialogue.

They all shared a short laugh, except for Faye Patterson, who spoke next.

"I have to agree with Mr. Lacy. She does not say she was raped by her father. She is the worst example of what rampant promiscuity in a woman can lead to."

Lacy smiled and seemed pleased that someone supported his viewpoint. At the same time, Jennifer Walsh shook her head before talking.

"It's hard to say what happened between her and her father. He was an extremely rich and powerful man, who wants, as he says, to buy the 'future.' He wants that future populated directly from his own demon seed. That's why he wants to have custody of the child, so he can control her, too. Mrs. Mulwray sees his evil, and wants to protect her daughter, like a caring mother."

There was more back and forth as to Mrs. Mulwray's behavior and the film's portrayal of it until Vince decided they should move on.

"Good discussion. And, as was pointed out, Mrs. Mulwray is a complicated figure, but, like a typical femme fatale, dies at the end, sort of as a punishment for her socially unacceptable sexuality. How about the character of Barbara in *I Want to Live!*?

"I don't think she was a femme fatale in the typical sense, but her sexual behavior is an important factor in the movie."

Evan spoke up in his usual formal manner.

"The film begins with a scene where there is a wild party taking place at which there is excessive drinking of alcohol. A band plays jazz (definitely the alternative sound of the time), and the musicians share a marijuana cigarette. The camera angles are skewed, emphasizing the out-of-the-ordinary lifestyles of those present. We first see Barbara rising from a bed in a slip, followed by the form of a man with whom she has slept for money. Thus, she is acting like a prostitute."

Vince could see Hope ready to deposit her two cents.

"Right from the start we see, like, how she helps men get away with crimes. She covers for the guy she slept with so he wouldn't be convicted of the Mann Act. The image of the bongo drums playing at the party are replaced by a judge's gavel as he convicts Barbara of prostitution, showing how society judges counterculture lifestyles. She later is totally maneuvered into providing an alibi for some crooked male friends, and is convicted of perjury. We know that men have physically abused her; her cigarette burns are evidence of that. There is a scene where one of the crooks is building a house of playing cards. It is so symbolic of Barbara's life, which comes tumbling down on her."

"Yeah, but she decides to do the wrong, not the right, thing," countered Lacy. "She falls in with some male criminals, and helps them fleece victims by seducing them. She also drives their getaway car after robberies, for Christ's sake."

"But she tries to leave that way of life by getting married and having a child," replied Hope.

"But, even though she tries to join the straight world, she continues to make the wrong choices," said Bill Herrman.

Jennifer Walsh joined the argument.

"But notice her problems come from relying on who? Men! And they pigeonhole women into playing limited roles. You have to be a wife, or a mother, or a spinster, or a whore. Society would label Barbara as a "party girl" and consider her a slut, but won't think of her as a mother, too. Just like men, she embraces her sexuality. For example, she refuses to wear the prison pajamas because she wants to feel sexy in her black slip. She strips and says she would rather be naked than wear drab clothes."

Vince decided to jump in.

"I think the movie shows Barbara's dual nature of being tough and independent, but also wanting to have a family. The film emphasizes her double-sided personality by showing her wanting to keep her daughter's stuffed toy, which happens to be a tiger, illustrating the sweet and dangerous sides of Barbara.

In any case, she eventually is framed for murder, and punished (in this case with the death penalty), like other movie female characters, for not playing a woman's prescribed societal role."

He paused before turning to other motion pictures.

"In *Chinatown* and *I Want to Live!* Both female lead characters suffer for their sexual transgressions. But there are films which show survival and vindication despite the women characters exercising their sexuality. In *The Last Seduction*, the character of Bridget is a modern femme fatale to the extreme. She is beautiful and very intelligent, and ruthless in getting what she wants. She uses men, through her sexuality, for her own gain. And, here, she gets away with it."

"I guess women can make men dizzy." said Goldman. "I mean look at *Vertigo*."

"We could spend a whole class just on Hitchcock's complicated portrayal of women," said Vince. "What do you think, Vern?"

Dr. Solomon nodded his head in agreement. Vince heard some muffled conversation between Lacy and Herrman.

"What was that, Ike?" asked Vince.

The two men glanced at each other, exchanging embarrassed smiles.

"Oh, are you talking to me? Sorry, couldn't resist. I was saying maybe a character like Travis Bickle from *Taxi Driver* would see all of these women we have been talking about as dirt he should clean up," said Lacy.

"Not sure about that," said Vince. "Bickle's a complex character when it comes to women. He is attracted to those who men have turned into sleazy porn stars, but, in a warped way, wants to save the world from its decay for a woman, played by Cybill Shepherd. And he wants to rescue the child prostitute played by Jodie Foster, possibly wanting to give her a chance to regain some of her youthful innocence. But you have offered me a segue, since Foster played the grown-up rape victim in *The Accused*. Anyone like to comment on that film?"

Lacy now appeared deflated at Vince's alternate opinion. Gina barely raised her hand, but Vince saw it.

"Yeah, Gina."

She looked at the others before speaking.

"I'm out of my league here, since I'm not into movies like all of you. But, I did see *The Accused*."

"Please tell us what you think," said Vince.

"I think the story shows that it doesn't matter if a woman comes from an upper-class or lower-class environment, she should be able to feel sexual without actually engaging in sex. Foster's character dances in a suggestive manner, but that doesn't mean it's a green light for a sexual assault. She says quite clearly that she doesn't want to be intimate, but, the men in the bar rape her. She goes to court to expose these men, and she is vindicated. The film reminds me of another movie on the subject, *North Country*."

"Well, Gina, you know more about films than you let on. There are films, like *North Country*, where there is the exploration of female sexuality, but where the woman requires a man to help her out of her imperiled situation. In *North Country*, she needs a male to testify as to the sexual harassment. Would anyone like to talk about another?"

Mark chose to interrupt his scrutiny of Bill Herrman and contribute to the meeting.

"In *Klute*, Jane Fonda's Bree is a prostitute who does not enjoy sex with her clients, and one of them, a sadistic killer, stalks her. It takes Donald Sutherland's Klute to open her up to sexual pleasure, because he is a caring man who is not there to exploit her. He also saves her from the killer at the end."

"I do think, let me see, how do I want to say this," said Goldman. "It should be pointed out that Bree enjoys the sexual power she exerts over her clients."

"That may be true," said Mark, "but given her situation, the only leverage men have allowed her was her sexual power, so in a sense, unlike men, her sexuality is the only part of her she can use to survive."

"That's ridiculous," argued Faye Patterson. "Women do not have to resort to prostitution to function in society. And those that do, warrant our scorn."

There was a short silence after Faye's angry outburst. Vince then spoke.

"What Faye says is true, in the sense that only a slight minority of women become professional prostitutes. Let's focus on the movie *Nuts*, in which Barbra Streisand's character is a high-priced call girl, and the film suggests that women, in some form or another, encounter men who treat them like whores. Martin Ritt directed this movie, and he also helmed *Norma Rae,* a film centering on female empowerment. I think *Nuts*, however, fits the class' topic. Here, Streisand's prostitute has killed one of her clients. The audience knows it was in self-defense. But, that is not the issue argued in the courtroom. It is whether she is competent to stand trial. Why do you think the film addresses this topic as opposed to her guilt or innocence?"

Debra Pearl's youthful energy seemed to get a fuel injection from the caffeine, as she again was the most exuberant hand waver.

"Rest your limb there, Debra. What do you have to say?" said Vince.

The twentysomething redhead spewed her answer almost in one breath.

"If guilt or innocence was the point of the story, it wouldn't matter what she did for a living, or whether it was a man or woman on trial. It's sorta like her nonconformist sexual activity is the focus. Her parents, and by association, society, believe that by choosing as her profession the oldest one, that she is mentally unfit. I could see how many people could say she is morally unfit, but mentally? If she is found incompetent to stand trial she won't even get a chance to prove her innocence. She'll, like, just be put away in a mental institution."

Vince nodded.

"Thank you, Debra. Good insight."

Goldman seemed not only to raise his hand but also his head in order to be recognized.

"Let's see what Joe has to say," said Vince, as he pointed to the young man as an invitation to speak.

"Well, *Nuts* has to do with males and females. Well, of course it would, given our theme. Let me see. Oh right! It's a double standard. I mean if we had a gigolo as the main character, he wouldn't be thought of being, ah, mentally unstable, right?"

Vince looked at Vernon, as if cueing his fellow instructor to speak next.

"Good point, ah, Mr., ah, that is, Joe. Anyway, to follow up on what was just said. I mean, when men have multiple sexual partners, it's expected, correct? But God forbid, and I, ah, mean that literally, if a woman is sexually promiscuous there must be something wrong with her, like she is a threat to society. But, Streisand's character is taught to give sex for money by her abusive stepfather. This action is an extreme version of what many girls were, and sometimes, still are, taught – look pretty and conform to the ideas of being the sought after sexual prize, and you will be rewarded with a house, cars, jewelry, furs, security. One might say that the film suggests that the typical role of a female is one of prostitution. So, in this movie there is, well, I would offer, an attempt by society to condemn the prostitute for exposing the reality behind the façade of society's version of love – that in the end it's a business transaction. Of course, let's hope many of us have evolved beyond that position."

After a little more talking about the Streisand film, Vince called for a ten-minute break. Those present formed little groups. Some talked about films, but Vince did hear worried conversation about what happened to Pauline Josephs. Vince steered away from those dealing with that topic. He joined Bill Herrman, James Player, and Ike Lacy as they snobbishly critiqued the casting of some actors in roles that they thought didn't work.

"Come on, having Marlon Brando play Marc Antony. Please!" said James. "I was ready to see him ride off on a motorcycle instead of a chariot."

"What about Charleton Heston playing a Mexican in *Touch of Evil*?" said Herrman. "He should have been deported back to the U.S. for fraud."

After they laughed, Vince said, "Well, they weren't importing a diverse collection of actors into Hollywood at that time, so give director Orson Welles a break."

After a short pause, Lacy offered his entry.

"I think that casting Dustin Hoffman in *Marathon Man* just didn't work. I mean, he's a shrimp, and he doesn't have that dark edge to be able to go up against a Nazi criminal and the American intelligence community."

Vince disagreed.

"Well, a lot of that movie has to do with appearances being deceptive. Look at the grandfatherly-looking Laurence Olivier who is really a murdering fascist. And, the spy, played by William Devane, pretends to be a good guy, but is a scary fellow. So Hoffman's character may look timid, but he is the marathon runner, the one standing at the finish line in the end."

While James and Bill nodded, Lacy wasn't convinced.

"I'd have made his brother, Roy Scheider's Doc, be the hero. He was the tough one. And, I would have killed off Hoffman's character, Levy."

Vince laughed, and said, "Well, that would have been a very different film."

"Yeah," said James. "It would be called 'Doc and the Nazi Dentist.'"

After more laughter, Vince resumed the class. They discussed other movies, including *Thelma and Louise*, which, Vernon argued, presented sexually liberated women fighting off the abusiveness of men, and driving away from them until they run out of road. Since they can't escape the exploitation of men, all that is left is a hand-clasped dive off a cliff.

The group talked for quite a while until Vince decided to end the discussion as The Bean Counter prepared to close. Vince was grateful for the chance to bring movies into the foreground of his thoughts, but he left the coffee house knowing that the menacing specter of death loomed in the background.

Chapter Thirty-eight

Thursday Night

The discussion at The Bean Counter adrenalized Vince and the movie geek gang, so they decided to hang out at Vince's house for a couple of hours after the class. They huddled in the family room, as they had done several times before, with Evan and Vernon Solomon seated on the sofa, Mark, James and Hope resting on throw pillows on the gray-carpeted floor, and Vince seated in his recliner. Gina came in to sit next to him in the rocker after ordering some pizza. Jellybean, who was hiding until the commotion of guests entering her sanctuary quieted down, emerged from behind a bookcase and jumped onto Vince's lap. She marked her territory, rubbing her face on either side of Vince's, and then pushed her head up against his, which was her way of showing affection.

"That is one terrific kitty you have there, Vince," said a smiling Mark. He then made some meow-like sounds. Jellybean jumped off of Vince and made herself comfortable in Mark's lap, accepting his chin scratches with squinting eyes.

"That's it," said Vince. "Suck up to the future vet. I think she's purring for free health care."

"Well, she's got it," said Mark, and then, in a cutesy voice to Jellybean, "Yes you do, you furry friend, yes you do."

"Get a kennel, you two, why don't you," said James.

"Well, I hope Mark won't be drinking Woolite out of a brown paper bag," said Hope.

"Whaaat?" said Gina.

Vince laughed.

"It's from Woody Allen's *Everything You Always Wanted to Know About Sex, (But Were Afraid to Ask)*," he said.

"It's told in episodes," said Evan. "There is one where Gene Wilder's character has a lamb for a mistress."

"And, ah, well, it doesn't go well, as you might guess," said Vernon, "and the last scene has him on skid row drinking ..."

And they all said at the same time, "Woolite out of a brown paper bag!"

"Wow," said Gina, "That's carrying affection for animals a little too far."

"Yes, you can love your pets, you just can't ... *love* your pets," said Mark.

"Line from *The Truth About Cats and Dogs*," said James and Evan almost simultaneously, followed by James saying, "delivered by Janeane Garofalo. I win."

"She plays a radio call-in veterinarian, so it's appropriate that Mark gave us the quote," said Evan to Gina.

"Okay, it's a tie, already!" said Hope. "Return to your neutral corners."

They continued to riff on a variety of films, even after the pizza arrived, speaking in between bites of traditional cheese and mushroom and white vegetable pies (Vince's favorite).

"Were you going to discuss *The Piano* in your class, Vince?" asked Mark.

"Yes," said Vince, "It's a significant movie, showing Holly Hunter's character exploring her sexuality in a positive way."

"But, she needs a male, Harvey Keitel's gone native New Zealand character, to bring out her passion," said Gina. "That's one I saw. I love that film."

Vince smiled and said, "Good observation.

He paused.

"A film we were going to highlight is Mike Nichols' *Working Girl*. Melanie Griffith's character is very sexual, but also has an extremely keen business mind. She is a complete woman."

"For sure. She's the one that says she has a mind for business and a bod for sin," said James.

"I don't know," said Hope. "She is gorgeous. And, the film exploits that to a degree by showing her vacuuming in the nude, modeling sexy lingerie. Maybe we need more stories about average looking females who represent the 'complete woman.'"

"Ah, well, we were going to finish with *The Contender*," said Vernon. "Joan Allen's character is up for the Vice-Presidential appointment following the death of the incumbent. She is attractive, but is not portrayed, ah, as you say, gorgeous, or glamorous. And she is very smart and admirable."

"Now you're talking," said Hope. "That film is underrated. It really attacks the double sexual standard. She can prove she wasn't involved in a group sex incident in college, but refuses to do so because if it's an irrelevant issue for a man, then it should be for a woman."

They focused on consuming more pizza before resuming the conversation.

"You know, Dad, you haven't mentioned *Looking for Mr. Goodbar* in the sessions. That is a film that shows a sexually promiscuous woman who attracts a disturbed male who winds up killing her."

"Not a very good movie, in my opinion," said Evan. "Looks like it's going to be a psychological study, but gets misogynistic."

"Sorta my point," said Hope. "It shows how a Hollywood movie doles out punishment for female sexual indulgence, which is not the case when films depict men as studs. I guess an argument could be made that it shows how sex can bring out the worst in the male gender, but the movie seems exploitative."

Vince shot a glance at Vernon, who nodded in response.

"Yeah, we talked about dealing with that one after the syllabus was distributed," said Vince. "But, as it turns out, after what happened to Kate Lawrence and Pauline Josephs, it's a good thing, given the violence against a sexually active woman in that film, that we didn't include it."

There was a wake-like silence that followed Vince's remarks. He appreciated Gina interrupting the quiet by changing the topic and the mood.

"How come current movies, and TV shows for that matter, many times start with a scene that shows characters in some kind of danger, then jump back in time. You know, you'll see a caption that says something like '72 hours earlier.'"

"Hello, it's a way of grabbing the audience's attention," said James. "With all the electronic distractions today, the filmmakers have to pull people quickly into the story so they don't start checking their cells."

"One of my pet peeves is telling people to start their 'two screen' experience when watching a TV show," said a testy Vince. "How can you concentrate on what you're watching when you're tweeting about the last scene you saw. Wait for the end of the program, people!"

"You have so many pet peeves, you could open up an animal shelter for them," said Hope with a laugh.

"The flashback after the opening has become a gimmick," said Evan, reverting to the original subject. "Everyone's doing it. The movie should build its story, providing incremental exposition as it goes along."

"My son, well, obviously, is not a fan of disjointed, out-of-sequence plots," said Vernon. "You're very traditional in some ways."

"Only in some," said Evan in a quiet voice.

"Guess *Memento* is not going to be at the top your movie charts," said Mark. "Kinda need to watch that one backwards to figure it out."

Vince started to say something about that movie, then stopped himself, and just stared. Gina noticed.

"Don't stifle yourself, you may strain something," said Gina, but Vince wasn't laughing.

"Backwards!" said Vince, as if the word should unlock hidden secrets.

He jumped out of the recliner, started pacing while grasping his face with his right hand, as if trying to extract the right words from his mouth.

"The clues at the last crime scene that didn't fit *Body Heat*," he said. "They refer to *The Last Seduction*."

"Sorry, I haven't seen that one," said Gina. "Can you fill me in?"

"The main character," said Vince, "is Bridget Gregory, played by Linda Fiorentino ..."

"Great performance," interrupted James, "and, she's really hot."

"James!" said Mark, "Not the point here, dude."

190

"Anyway," said Vince, "she's in an illegal drug business with her prescription writing doctor husband, Clay ..."

"Played by Bill Pullman," interrupted Evan.

"Right. And she gets pissed off at him for smacking her, so she takes the money and runs," said Vince.

"Yeah, she pulls a Woody Allen," said Hope. After Gina looked at her and raised questioning hands, she added, "You know, Allen's movie, *Take the Money and Run.*"

Gina rolled her eyes.

"Anyway," said Vince. "Bridget, trying to hide her identity so her husband won't find her, changes her name to Wendy Kroy, which is ..."

"Great Vince!" said Vernon. "Ah, Bridget can automatically write words backwards, so if you drop the 'dy' off of Wendy, and you reverse the letters, you get 'New.'"

"And 'Kroy' is 'York' spelled backwards," said Hope. "She comes from New York, and doesn't like the small town she has to hide out in."

Gina nodded her head to reflect her understanding.

"And that's why Pauline's name was spelled backwards on the fake will in her apartment," she said.

"Exactly," said Vince. "The killer pointed us to *The Last Seduction.* Bridget wore tight, short skirts and black stockings, which is what Pauline was wearing when the police found her. And, now, the can of Mace makes sense."

"Because," said Evan, following up on Vince's thought, "Bridget/Wendy goes back and kills her husband with it, framing her new patsy boyfriend, Mike."

"That's why the killer placed Pauline's body on the couch," said Hope in a quiet, shaky voice. "That's where Bridget killed Clay."

"And, *The Last Seduction* fits the pattern," added Vince. "It, along with *Basic Instinct* and *Body Heat*, have seductive femme fatales getting away with murder. Our killer is re-writing the endings of those movies to fit his, or her, version of justice."

Gina simply said, "Wow."

Hope, after lowering her head as if saying a prayer for Pauline, raised it, and said, "But ..."

"I know," said Vince. "We still don't know the significance of the DVD. What does *Hush, Hush, Sweet Charlotte* have to do with all of this?"

Chapter Thirty-nine

Friday morning

Vince agreed to talk with Lt. Harvey Douglas at the precinct headquarters on this stormy end of the work week day, but he wasn't singing in the rain about it. Although he agreed with Douglas that the murderer should continue to see Vince's participation in the cases, he did not appreciate it slipping out to the press that he was visiting the police department. The media people were waiting like *Jurassic Park* raptors ready to pounce on Vince. He ploughed through the crowd just saying that he was willing to help the authorities, but other than that he had no comment.

Once inside the building, he flipped back the hood on his water-resistant jacket (he disliked carrying umbrellas, especially when the wind blew them inside out and you felt like an embarrassed Mary Poppins). A uniformed officer escorted Vince to Douglas' office. He found the lieutenant sitting sideways in his chair, staring out of the picture window while he absentmindedly stirred the black coffee in the mug on the desk. Vince was a bit startled when Douglas spoke, in his Tommy Lee Jones monotone speech pattern, because it didn't appear that he realized that Vince was present.

"Have any problem with the reporters?" Douglas asked.

Vince took off his jacket, hung it on the back of the chair facing Douglas' desk, and sat down.

"Other than having to fullback my way through them, no," was Vince's response.

"Well, knowing that you most likely have seen *Friday Night Lights*, you knew what to do. Want some coffee?" said Douglas with no pause between sentences.

Vince made a wincing face as he looked at the murky liquid in Douglas' mug.

"Not unless you can whip up a white chocolate mocha."

"This isn't a Starbucks, Singleton," said Douglas, with a head shake. "So, what have you got for me?"

Vince laid out how he felt the clues suggested that the next murder would revolve around the film *The Last Seduction.*

"Hmm," said Douglas, as he seemed to consider what Vince had told him. "But, all we know is maybe why these killings are taking place, how most of the clues fit into this misogynistic pattern. But, you haven't been able to figure out who the next victim will be."

Vince shook his head in the negative.

"Can't tell me anything else?" asked Douglas, Vince hearing impatience in his voice.

Vince started to get a little peeved. At least he saw how the evidence fit together, and the motive behind the murders. That was more than what the cops had accomplished.

"No," he said, "But maybe you could tell *me* something for a change. Like, what have you learned about the people your department has been investigating."

Douglas took a slurp from his mug, and then let out a loud sigh.

"Well," he said, "several of the members in your film class don't have alibis on the nights of the killings.

You know, home alone, watching TV or streaming something. Some played video games, others read or exercised. The typical solitary activities of our times."

Douglas paused and took another sip of the dark brew.

"You know about Faye Patterson's anger towards you and Cassandra Kimble. And, her interview showed hostility towards what she would consider sexually overactive women, including Kate Lawrence, and Pauline Josephs. I already told you about Bill Herrman's female cyber bullying charge. Patterson was alone in her house on the nights of the killings. Herrman was in his apartment by himself during the first attack, and he says he was at a movie theater when the second murder took place, but he went alone, and doesn't think anyone would recognize him."

"What about Ike Lacy? He knew Josephs," said Vince.

Douglas opened a folder on his desk and quickly skimmed its contents.

"Mr. Lacy likes to talk, mostly about himself. He's thirty-one years old, and grew up near Altoona, Pennsylvania. Said he was an orphan who didn't know his birth parents, and never felt the need to find out who they were. The couple that raised him died in a car accident after he graduated college. Works as a freelance book editor and an aspiring actor. Arrived in Philly just under a year ago. Says he lived in New York City for a while, but it was hectic there with too much competition to land any parts in plays. Why Philly? Likes cheesesteaks, and always wanted to live near the Rocky steps. His apartment is just off the Ben Franklin Parkway, so that dream came true. Occupation and address checked out. We're working on the rest of his background. He has a Facebook page which has lots of posts about acting, but not many head shots. I think his prospects are like mine if I ever tried to get into the movies – no romantic leads, just character roles."

Vince barked out a quick laugh at the line. Douglas continued.

"Takes a lot of movie classes. That's where he met Pauline Josephs, at one offered by the Dilworth Library in Conshohocken. He told me he signed up for your class because he liked the theme."

"Well, that statement could cut both ways," said Vince.

"My thoughts exactly," said Douglas. "He also said he wasn't with anybody on the nights of the killings."

He shuffled through more files.

"I'm supposed to put all of this on the computer. I'm still enrolled in the old school of record keeping."

After a moment, he spoke again.

"Talked with Joe Goldman. Thirty-two years of age. Writes his own movie blog about mysteries and horror films. He's a substitute teacher. He is a big fan of yours. Kept talking about your book and online commentary. Kept saying that he hoped you liked his comments on your blog, and his dream was to collaborate with you somehow. Again, no alibis."

"Yeah, that sounds a bit creepy. If he's the murderer, then maybe he sees my participation in the case as a kind of collaboration," said Vince.

"Thought crossed my mind," said Douglas, appearing distracted while scanning his computer screen after abandoning his paper files.

"Interviews of those you mentioned who showed up at the coffee shop were conducted by detectives working on the case before last evening. Their reports are in the database. Let's see. Jennifer Walsh. Thirty-five. Divorced. Husband left her for what she described as his sexy female accounting business partner. Seemed bitter that her spouse neglected her and never wanted children, and she is seeing a psychologist for depression. No alibis."

"She might have been warped into thinking that sexy women undermine females like her who play the wife role," said Vince. He was feeling desperate to find the culprit.

Douglas clicked on the computer mouse.

"Maybe. Jeffrey Shestack. Fifty-five years old. He was never married, takes care of his invalid mother, does audits for the IRS. Says he was home with his mom on the days in question, but his mother has dementia, and can't verify the information."

"Mother issues? A lifetime of parental devotion caused him to not know how to relate to women?" said Vince.

Douglas didn't comment.

"Debra Pearl. Twenty-five. Works as a wedding planner. Says she was working late at night on her home laptop on the dates of the killings. We checked it out, and her computer was in use, but we don't know if it was she who was using it or not."

"Well, femme fatales would not be on her client list," said an exasperated Vince. "We're running out of time. We have to come up with something soon, before this killer exacts more deranged justice by rewriting movie plots."

"Then, you and your film fanatics better get to work and come up with something," said Douglas.

Chapter Forty

Friday Afternoon

Jake arrived at the small public playground in Northeast Philadelphia on Welsh Road just west of the Roosevelt Boulevard. He was a bit out of sorts because he had skipped his usual Greek yogurt for lunch to allow himself more time in case he became lost while driving to the location. As he got out of his air-conditioned car, the summer heat slammed into him, opening up his pores, enabling the sweat to leak out in short order. He took off his sports jacket and threw it into the back seat of the Prius, vaguely thinking that his car was getting old, and he should look into buying one of those totally electric vehicles. He checked the battery life on his tiny digital recorder. He hoped he would get something useful on the record from Nancy Dahl.

Jake had called Linda York's friend several times, leaving phone messages without receiving any answers. He kept reassuring her that he wasn't a policeman or from some collection agency. He gave her the phone number of his newspaper editor so that she could check him out. Still no response. Finally, he asked Linda's sister, Barbara, to give Nancy a call to pave the way for the meeting. He finally received a message from the woman to set up this appointment. She sounded shaky on the phone, and hung up quickly.

As he walked toward the seesaw, slide and sandbox area, he saw Nancy, wearing the red Ocean City New

Jersey hat she said would identify her. She was sitting alone on a bench close to where young children were playing. As he walked toward her, he noticed mothers and fathers off to the side, talking and smiling, but with their heads turned toward their offspring, trying to ensure that the little boys and girls would be safe. As Jake approached Nancy, he saw that she had dressed for the heat by wearing jean shorts and a light blue tank top. Her large sunglasses covered her eyes, but her head darting back and forth showed that she was checking for any signs of danger. Despite the hat and glasses, he could see that she was an attractive woman. There was a bottle of Pepsi and a large black purse on the bench next to her.

"Nancy Dahl?"

"Sit down!" Nancy said in a hushed voice, as she looked around. "Make like you're watching one of your kids playing."

Jake did as he was told. He sat back on the bench, crossed his leg, trying to appear relaxed. He looked over at the children playing after glancing at the tense woman seated next to him, her arms wrapped around her trunk, as if trying to protect herself in human body armor. She looked frightened, but that just made the reporter in him more interested.

"Why are you so afraid, Nancy?"

She gave out a loud sigh and peeked at him over her sunglasses.

"You'd be scared, too, if you were a black woman whose black friend was killed by some crazy-ass white cop!"

Jake thought, *Now we're getting to the good stuff.*

"I thought her boyfriend, Leon, killed Linda."

Nancy shook her head from side to side.

"No way that boy hurt Linda. It was that big ol' policeman that did it. I know. Linda told me about him. I was her best friend. I know. But, I'm not telling you nothin' unless you don't mention my name. If you do, I'll deny everything, and point that bastard at you if he finds me."

Jake could hear Nancy's voice crack when she said, "best friend." He thought it was time to show that he wasn't just after a story at her expense. The main reason he became a reporter was to get at the truth, so people would be empowered by it, and they could a make a difference.

"I promise you, you won't be mentioned. I want to get whoever killed Linda. I think it was the same person who has something to do with the death of my sister-in-law. You help me, and I will try to get justice for the both of us."

Nancy looked down at the ground for what seemed to Jake like several minutes. He watched the children going up and down on the seesaw for a bit. When he turned back to the woman, it was hard to tell behind the sunglasses whether or not she had dozed off. But then Nancy nodded her head a couple of times as if showing that she had made up her mind, and she began to speak.

"Now, Linda was a good girl. She always was nice to people, would babysit her friends' kids. We met when she was still going to college, before all that bad stuff went down about her father and mother. I was going through a divorce and a custody fight for my little girl at the time. Linda was always there for me. We would go to the movies. Sometimes she would visit when I was down and we would watch silly TV shows together. We took long walks, talked about our families, friends, men."

Nancy paused and gave herself another hug.

"Anyway, when she crashed after what went down with her parents, she took up with Leon, and started with the drugs. I tried to help her, but I'm no professional counselor. Barbara let me know that she told you how that Detective Campbell caught Linda when she was selling coke for Leon. Well, that cop used her. Now, she never talked about Leon's crimes, but she did give up other people who sold drugs. Campbell said if she didn't give him information, he would send her away for a long time. At first, he gave her things, but later, he made her have sex with him. Linda said he was rough, too. He told Linda that he would hurt her and her sister if she said anything about what he was doing."

Nancy pulled off her sunglasses and for the first time since Jake arrived, she looked him in the eyes.

"Campbell started complaining about having to see a psychologist after he was involved in a shooting. He used to get drunk at Linda's place and one time he said something like, 'That goddamn Singleton woman's got no right to keep grilling me, making me come back about that shooting.' Linda said once he was at her place with this stocky cop by the name of Smartley. They were talking about the shooting. At this particular meeting, Smartley said 'Well, they can't trace that gun I gave you to plant on the guy, so it's got to look like you had a righteous kill.' And Campbell said he placed the gun right in the hands of the fella he shot, so the case should be closed. He continued to complain about Dr. Singleton, saying, 'Her name may be Jewel, but she ain't worth a damn as a woman. She's not bad looking, but gets hostile if you say something nice about her legs.' If she didn't clear him of the shooting, he said, according to Linda, he would have to, 'put a hurt on her.' From what Linda said that Smartley wasn't too thrilled by the idea, but after Campbell reminded him that he owed Campbell, Smartley said he would do whatever had to be done. So, Linda tracked Jewel Singleton down. She thought maybe if she told her what a bad policeman he was, Singleton could write something up, bring him down, and he wouldn't find out it was Linda who was behind it."

Nancy picked up the Pepsi, which Jake figured must have lost its quench factor in the heat, and took a small sip.

"She actually met with this Jewel Singleton several times, because the psychologist wanted to help her with her drug problem. She did it for free, too. Linda told Dr. Singleton that Campbell raped her and threatened to hurt her sister. Linda told her about Smartley, too. It's all in the records. She also warned Dr. Singleton that Campbell didn't like the way she was giving him a tough time about that shooting. Linda told me Dr. Singleton was preparing to expose Campbell. But, maybe because Linda was basically an honest person, and lying came so unnatural to her, Campbell became suspicious of her when she didn't have consistent stories about where she had been and what she was doing. He must have followed her, and found out that she was seeing Dr. Singleton. I'm sure he killed Linda, and that is why I heard that Jewel Singleton's office was broken into, and records stolen, and that good woman was murdered, too. When you said your name was Singleton, too, I decided to meet with you."

Jake thought about what Nancy said, and it confirmed what Vince had suspected. But, it was just Nancy's word against that of an ex-policeman. And Nancy didn't want to be named as an informant.

"I want to thank you for being brave enough to meet me and tell me what happened. I will pass it on to someone who will keep trying to have Campbell pay for what he did. But, all we have is your story. I can't promise you the justice you want."

Nancy grabbed the large handbag and placed it on her lap.

"Linda suspected that Campbell might try to get hold of her patient records from Dr. Singleton. So, she asked her to print out Linda's file, which has all the dirt about Campbell, and give it to her, and not keep any physical copies or computer records. She was a smart girl."

Nancy pulled out a folder and showed Jake documents and a cell phone that were inside it.

"Now Linda figured she needed to get something on Campbell to get free of him. So, she used her old cell to record stuff. There's recordings that show how Campbell and Smartley talked about how they might take down Dr. Singleton. She gave it and the records to me because Campbell didn't know about little old Nancy here. Maybe you can use these to stop that man from ever hurting anybody else."

Chapter Forty-one

Friday Night

Vince used to like the evening. When he taught English in the public schools, he enjoyed coming home and relaxing with his family after finishing the day's last class and preparing for subsequent lessons. He and Jewel told Hope to always treat herself to something enjoyable each day, even if it was just a walk, a conversation with a friend, or watching a favorite TV show or movie. Jewel made those little moments special, with her sense of humor, her smile, her intelligence. She was an amplifier of life. And these policemen, the ones who were supposed to protect her special gifts, had conspired to quiet her beautiful voice. They left Vince with nightmarish revisitings of the horrific scene where bullets tore his wife's body beyond repair. So, Vince was anything but tranquil as he listened with Jake and Newman to the tape his brother acquired from Nancy Dahl. He was grateful that Gina and Hope had gone out for sushi, because he didn't want either of them to see how agitated he was.

"You have to nail these bastards, Ray! You can hear from their own words on that recorder that they worked together to murder someone even before Jewel. They'll do it again. Especially that Campbell. He'll kill again. You know he will."

"I know, Vince, I know," said Newman. "Let me just take a look at Jewel's records of Linda York's sessions with her."

As Newman scanned the documents while sitting on the sofa, and Jake occupied the rocker with the purring Jellybean in his lap, Vince paced the room, empathizing with how Cassandra must feel confined in her jail cell. After Newman finished his review, he spoke.

"Linda said some very incriminating things here about Campbell, especially how he raped the poor woman, repeatedly. And, we have written and recorded evidence that he threatened to hurt Jewel. I think we have enough here that points to Campbell killing Linda York and deliberately shooting Jewel. And, since I reopened the case involving the death of your wife, I believe it's Campbell and Smartley who have attempted to frame me, trying to make it seem that I'm involved in the current killings. It looks like we have enough to move against them. I'll meet with Douglas first since I believe the two investigations are now linked. Personally, as a policeman, I'm deeply ashamed that these men have anything to do with my profession."

Vince nodded his head and finally sat down in his recliner. Jellybean, instinctively sensing that her human companion needed her, jumped off of Jake's lap and onto Vince's. She began rubbing her face on either side of Vince's, reminding him that he was her special person. Vince allowed himself a slight smile and stroked Jellybean's smooth fur.

"Jake, you don't think we can get Nancy to testify?" asked Newman.

Jake shook his head.

"I doubt it. She is super frightened of Campbell. She made me paranoid. I'm looking over my shoulder now everywhere I go. Can you blame her? No offense, Lieutenant, but back in the day, when I was protesting against the Vietnam War, the cops were pretty brutal against anybody they considered a threat to their way of doing things. I mean, where do you turn, or hide, when those with the power are out to get you?"

"Okay, Jake, you have a point, but we're all on the same side in this room," said Vince, "and right now we're just trying to go after these two men."

Jake raised both hands with palms outward in a ceasefire gesture.

Vince looked at Newman.

"But Ray, Jake's paranoia has merit. Watch your back."

Newman offered a tight smile.

"Already got it covered," he said.

Chapter Forty-two

Early Saturday Morning

Patrick Campbell sat in a Chevy Impala he had rented under a fake ID. He figured he better be careful when dealing with a cop, even if it was a snot-nosed rookie. He had pulled into the parking lot of Newman's apartment building before dawn. Not likely there would be much activity early on a Saturday morning. He drank some black coffee he had poured from the thermos. He always made his own brew. Those fools who bought their high-priced lattes were getting robbed. Not him.

He took another gulp, and thought that he had to give Smartley credit. His old army buddy had checked the surveillance logs and read that Newman had been showing up at the Singleton address. Smart-Ass (which is what Campbell liked to call Smartley when he wanted to push his old pal's buttons) was right about the need to keep an eye on Newman. Campbell started following him, and sure enough, there he was at Singleton's place last night. Campbell had parked a secure distance from the house. He wished he had Singleton's place bugged so he could know what those two were hatching up. What surprised him was the appearance of Jake Singleton. When the brother left his car, Campbell saw that he was carrying something. He grabbed his infrared telephoto lens to see what it was. It looked like a document folder used in an office. Campbell knew that Singleton used his brother to gather information on Cassandra Kimble in California, outside of Newman's jurisdiction. Since Newman was suspended, were they using Jake again?

Campbell hadn't liked what he saw, and he really didn't like what he saw later. When Newman walked out of the house he was carrying the same folder that Jake Singleton had brought into the house. Campbell's police instinct, (once a cop, always a cop), told him that that file may be the missing one from Jewel Singleton's office, the one that contained whatever that damn bitch Linda had told the psychologist about him. He knew he had to get hold of that file.

He didn't tell Smartly what he saw, and what he was planning. His old friend was loyal, but sometimes he didn't know when was the right time to pull the trigger. He would have tried to work some roundabout, complicated scheme to slow Newman down. There wasn't time for that. Campbell knew he had to act.

Campbell came to attention as he saw Newman exit the door to his building. Sure as shit, he was carrying that same folder. He was going to get that file off of Newman before he could bring it into the Department. He grabbed the gun with the silencer out of the glove compartment and put it into his pocket. So what if he took the goods off of Newman? If questioned, he would say that it was bunk, that Newman was suspended for being a suspect in the killings, and he and the Singletons were just blowing smoke to get the cops off Newman's back. He moved quickly, took the gun out of his pocket, and snuck up behind Newman as he reached his car.

"Don't try anything," Campbell whispered to Newman. "You're going to hand that package over."

"Don't be a fool," said Newman. "If you hurt me, it's your ass that's going to burn."

"I don't think so," said Campbell. "If I have to shoot, I'll put you in the trunk of your car, and drive you over to my neighborhood. I have a gun to plant on you, and I'll say it was self-defense, that you were stalking me. Now hand it over."

Campbell heard a footstep behind him. He spun around and a quick recognition pushed a door open in his memory. He started to aim his gun, but the man in front of him was faster and his weapon exploded. Campbell felt an impact and intense pain in his chest. He fell to the ground. The last words he heard came from Newman yelling, "Are you okay, Dad?"

Chapter Forty-three

Saturday Evening

Newman observed Detective Ben Smartley handcuffed to the table in the station's interrogation room. His usual arrogant smirk was gone. His broad shoulders were sagging. Actually, Newman thought, his whole body looked like it had suffered a cave-in. Newman glanced over at the other person in the room, Harvey Douglas. Newman had to admit it, Douglas moved fast on this one. After he called in Campbell's shooting, the police brought him and his dad in for questioning. Newman turned over the evidence to Douglas and filled him in on what was going on. Douglas was none too pleased with Newman's private investigation, officially, but privately, he commended him on what he accomplished, along with the help of Jake Singleton. He said he was sure that after required protocol had been followed, Newman's father would be released since he killed Patrick Campbell in self-defense.

Douglas contacted a judge, who issued a warrant, and he marched right into the office to arrest Smartley, who was mad as hell at first, cursing everyone in sight. Once he heard what went down with his old Army pal, and that the evidence showed he was involved in committing multiple felonies, including covering up murders, he shut up.

"I contacted Nancy Dahl. She was Linda York's friend. You didn't know about her, did you Smartley?"

Newman said to him shortly after the arrest. "Linda kept her a secret, along with Jewel Singleton's records, and recordings of Campbell and you. Nancy's the one who gave them to us. And, now that Campbell is dead, she is not afraid to testify. She will state what Linda told her, and confirm that Nancy received the evidence from her." After that, Smartley gave up the fight. He even refused to have a lawyer present during the interrogation. He also disclosed the names of the two ex-cons that were part of the set-up at Jewel Singleton's murder.

Douglas looked at the broken man in front of them before speaking.

"I thought you were more intelligent than this, Smartley," he said. "Were you really all in on your buddy's plans?"

Smartley shook his head a couple of times.

"Campy always did shoot from the hip. Sometimes it worked. Like when he had my back in the war. But here, not so much. I had to bat cleanup. Didn't know he was going to kill the York and Singleton women. He did tell me how he framed Linda York's boyfriend. But, I sure as hell didn't think he would try to strong-arm Newman. I did break into Jewel Singleton's office to steal the records. And, it was my idea to set up Newman, to get him off Campbell's back."

"Why, Smartley? Why did you go so far down this road?" asked Douglas.

Smartley chuckled.

"Campy saved my life. And others. It's hard to say no to someone you've known so long and gone to war with. But, I would be lying if I said I wasn't relieved to know it's over."

Newman, who had been leaning against the wall, straightened up.

"It's just starting for you, Smartley," he said. "And I'm outta here. I'm going to see my dad."

***

Newman wandered over to booking where Pete Singleton was being processed. The atmosphere there was relaxed. His father was actually laughing with some of the men surrounding him.

"Hey, son. I was just jawing with these guys. Told about that time we were chasing this punk around the Ninth Street Market. We happened to be there when he stole this woman's purse. He grabbed some bananas and started throwing them back at us, hoping we would slip on the peels, I guess. I picked up on his idea and bopped him with a cantaloupe. Sprawled him out on the sidewalk. Guess he brought a banana to a melon fight."

There was renewed laughter.

"Yeah, yeah. I heard that one before," said Newman. "You guys mind if I have a little time with my father, here?"

"Naw, go ahead," said a Detective Billings, a young fellow who had been one of the first to arrive at the scene at Newman's apartment building. "But, I don't think he'll be using our accommodations here for too long. Nice meeting you, Pete."

His father gave the man a wave as he and the others scattered.

"Have some coffee and a donut, son," said his father as he took a bite from a Boston Cream.

Newman saw his dad look at the boxes of donuts and coffee pot in front of them.

"Yeah, getting treated better than when I left this joint. Guess you have to keep at doing the right thing before it pans out."

Newman smiled and, never one to pass up food, grabbed a jelly donut and took a big bite. They both drank some coffee.

"You were right about how dangerous it can be when you're messing with crooked cops. It was a good idea that you offered to tail me," said Newman.

"I do know something about problems with dishonest policemen," said his father. "And, it was good that you *let* me back you up."

"I admit I had to take a beat before saying yes. I was worried about you getting burned because of me."

Pete put his arm around his son.

"We're family. We fight the fire together."

Newman laughed.

"Okay, we're cops. Enough with the firemen metaphors."

"Well, I'm an ex-cop, but today, I felt like I was making a difference again."

"You always make a difference for me, Pop," said Newman as he patted his father on the back.

Chapter Forty-four

Sunday Morning

The day's weather was promising, with the temperature only reaching around eighty degrees. Vince looked up at the bright sky. His mood, however, reflected a darker blue than the shade painted above him. Despite finding out that the man who killed Jewel was dead, and those who conspired with him would be brought to justice, Vince could not push back the emptiness he felt inside. While he had sought those responsible for her death, he had been able to keep at bay the pain of losing his wife. Now, those waves of sorrow washed over him again.

Gina held his hand as they walked around the suburban streets close to Vince's house. She kept looking over at him, obviously sensing his melancholy mood since he had been silent for a while.

"What are you thinking?" she asked.

"About how stupid TV commercials have become. Did you see that asthma one that says it has more ingredients than other products, and it's better because '6 is greater than 1?' Gee, thanks for reminding me. I kept forgetting that mathematical fact. And what about the ad that says its food product contains 'real' ingredients. As opposed to what, imaginary ones?"

Gina smiled, but didn't let him get off that easy.

"Tell me something about Jewel."

Vince smelled something cooking on a grill as they passed a split-level house on their right, and it brought back a memory.

"She used to make this terrific Hawaiian chicken dish. She would chop up pieces of the bird and put them in a skillet with pineapples, mix in some orange juice, and add carrots, tomatoes, cinnamon, and some other stuff I don't remember. Anyway, it would cook for quite a while, and the chicken became real tender, and she would serve it over rice. I can almost smell it right now."

"Didn't you help with the meal?" she asked.

"I was the one who made sure all of the pans, plates, bowls, and silverware were ready to use. And, I would do all the washing up afterward. I did all the cleaning around the house, the laundry. It was a good division of labor. We meshed pretty well."

They were quiet again for a short time before Gina spoke again.

"Vince, why do you think Jewel didn't say something about Campbell once Linda York was found dead?"

"I asked Newman about that. Looks like everything happened fairly close together. From what they discovered from the entry dates in Jewel's notes, and what Nancy Dahl told the police, Jewel gave Linda her records and said she would make them available once Jewel contacted someone she could trust in Internal Affairs at the police department. But Campbell was already onto Linda, and killed her, but after she had given her records to her friend, Nancy. Then, there was the break-in to steal Jewel's records that Campbell and Smartley didn't know had been removed. Campbell targeted Jewel before Linda's body was even found, so she didn't have a chance to point the police at Campbell."

Gina sighed and squeezed Vince's arm.

"At least it's over, now," she said.

Vince echoed her sigh before speaking.

"That horror story may be done, but we have a double feature, and the second story isn't finished yet."

Chapter Forty-five

Monday Morning

Hope felt that combination of sadness and satisfaction that music can conjure as she listened to Green Day's "Boulevard of Broken Dreams" playing on Mark's iPhone as they sat on the living room sofa. She settled deeper into the safe nook under Mark's right shoulder and next to his firm side, as his arm encircled her clinging form.

"You're going to be a vet, and you don't even have any animals in here. Not even a hamster. What's with the mixed messages, fella?"

Mark kissed her on the forehead.

"Don't blame me. It's because of James and his allergies. Living with that guy can sometimes put a detour in the road."

"I thought the truth was just cats and dogs he couldn't be around? Does he also have a problem with Janeane Garofalo, too?"

"Didn't we already use that film reference recently? And, I think he would endure hives for Uma Thurman. But, seriously, I think he may even be allergic to air."

They both laughed.

"So, any chance you might be moving out before Social Security kicks in?" asked Hope.

"Not too long before school is over with. That job at the veterinarian's office your dad set me up with will help bring in some coin."

"Well, current events have put up a roadblock in my apartment hunting. But, hopefully we will eventually get some privacy without you having to put a sock on the doorknob to let James know you're, ah, boning up on your studies."

They laughed again. Mark was quiet for a minute, and Hope looked up at his thoughtful face.

"Whatcha thinking about?" she asked.

"You know, even though I like to kid about James, he's okay. I mean, just like you and me, we talk movies a lot. Let's face it, most of the world thinks we're just weirdos. And me, with my animal rights thing, most of the people I know say, oh, why don't you lighten up already, and party while you can. And James, he's like an orphan, in a way, with how he's always sort of eclipsed by all the attention his parents get."

Hope understood. She knew that empty feeling that she shared with Mark since his dad and her mom were taken away from them. It sort of set them apart, even if it was in their own minds, from most of the young people they knew.

The knob to the front door began to turn, and James and Evan walked in.

"Dude, no foot apparel on the door, so I figured it was cool to enter," said James.

"No problem," said Mark. "We were just making lame allusions to *The Truth About Cats and Dogs.*"

"Not that movie again," said Evan.

"Hey, I like that one. Funny flick. And, Uma Thurman is so hot in it," said James.

Mark swiveled his head toward Hope and said, "See what I mean?"

"What?" said James.

"Yes, it's entertaining, but it reinforces female stereotypes," said Evan. "Thurman's character is the gorgeous dumb blonde, and Garofalo plays the runty smart one."

"Oh, come on, Evan," said Hope. "In the end, cute Ben Chaplin's photographer, who is used to just seeing pretty faces, picks the unglamorous Garofalo. See, true beauty lies within."

"Really, have you ever really looked at Uma Thurman?" said James.

"Down boy," said Mark.

"If the movie was saying looks don't matter, then why is the good-looking man the prize? It's a cop-out," said Evan. "Anyway, I need some restroom relief."

As Evan headed for the bathroom, Hope looked at James.

"Why is he extra grumpy?" she whispered.

After Evan closed the bathroom door, James leaned forward.

"He came out to his mom yesterday," he said. "I think he felt empowered after we were so encouraging once he told us. His father went with him, sort of a supporting actor bit. Let's just says the news didn't elicit a rave review from her. She started to blame his dad for not being a strong enough role model, you know, not butch enough, or whatever. Guess she hasn't heard of Lady Gaga's 'Born This Way.'"

Both Hope and Mark shook their heads in disappointment. Hope could see that Evan noticed their sad faces when he joined them.

"So, you told them," he said to James.

"Look, man, I'm sorry. I just ..."

"It's okay," said Evan. "I was going to say something anyway. If I can't talk it over with you guys, then who?"

Hope smiled, relieved that Evan was loosening up his uptightness for his friends.

"Listen Evan, time is on your side," she said. "She'll come around."

Evan smiled.

"Yeah, but I think she may take the long way to get there."

Chapter Forty-six

Monday Afternoon

Vince hadn't watched a double feature in a while, and there was little elastic left in his stiff middle-aged legs after the marathon viewing of *The Last Seduction* and *Hush, Hush ... Sweet Charlotte*. He rose up from the rocker, whose ghostly continuing sways moved quicker than did he as he walked with achiness around his family room. Hope stretched herself leisurely on the recliner, which, out of tradition, he always let her use when they watched films or TV shows together. She twisted a curl of her long brown hair around her right index finger, a habit she adopted when in contemplative thought. Gina sat at an angle on the couch to the right of the rocker, one leg on and the other off the furniture. She was motion picture endurance challenged, and had dozed off a few times.

"Okay, any insights?" asked Gina. "And, just to show that I didn't totally phase out, I thought it was very upsetting that one of the characters in *Hush, Hush ... Sweet Charlotte* was named Jewel. But, I don't think that can be construed as a threat."

"No, but it may be meant to scare me by making it personal," said Vince, who had forgotten this fact, and experienced a visceral chill when he heard Jewel's name in the movie.

Hope put a few more twists in the curl before speaking.

"Yeah, but this film doesn't really fit in with the whole femme fatale theme of the other flicks. The Jewel character we find out killed her husband, but because he was cheating on her. And Charlotte did the two people in who were scheming against her. These women are not like the creepy, scheming women in *Basic Instinct*, *Body Heat*, or *The Last Seduction*."

Vince's hair wasn't long enough to finger-twirl, so he did his own male version of ruminating by stroking a hand over his jaw.

"Yeah, you're right. I don't see an obvious connection. Let's stick with the other film, since that one fits the pattern. The killer wants me to play the game of figuring out the clues, and we saw that he left a hint at who the next victim would be at the first crime scene. He probably did it again at the second."

They were quiet for a while as each one of them became lost in their own thoughts. Gina stirred the stillness with a question.

"What about the way Bridget twisted words around? What did she do again?"

Hope looked at Vince before talking.

"She wrote them backwards."

"Yeah, what's with that? Could there be something there?" asked Gina.

"Could be, could be," said Vince, his voice barely audible. "The killer did do some wordplay with the 'pj' abbreviation for pajamas, standing for Pauline Joseph's name."

He went into the living room and returned with a pen and some paper. He started to write names down.

"So, we have Linda Fiorentino playing this badass Bridget Gregory," he said. "I see 'get gory' in the character's name. Not a person, so no help."

"There's a 'rory,' but I don't think there's anybody with that name that flicks a switch," said Gina.

"The word 'Bride" is in the first name," said Hope. "We don't know anybody who was recently married. And, it's not likely a reference to Uma Thurman's character, Beatrix, in the *Kill Bill* movies. She kills men and women both who left her for dead, so those films are revenge stories. And I can't think of anyone going by her character's unique name."

"Right. We have to focus on the belief that the killer wants to take out women who he sees as femme fatales to make up for the women who got away with their crimes in the movies he is referencing," said Vince.

He pointed to the next name he wrote.

"How about Mike Swale, played by Peter Berg, the man Bridget seduces and uses to get back at her husband. Can we pull anything out of that?" asked Vince.

Gina stared at the paper.

"Well, at this point, I could go for some 'ale,'" she said.

"Even I can OD on thinking about movies," said Hope, rubbing her eyes. "I have a headache. Maybe we should bring in the movie geek cavalry, and get the Solomon's, James, and Mark over here."

Vince kept staring at the paper with the character names written on it.

"Hey Jodie Foster, should I make *Contact* with the others?" asked Hope, addressing Vince.

Vince reluctantly interrupted his scrutiny.

"What? Ha, Jodie Foster, huh? Yeah, you're 'okay to go,'" he said.

Gina shook her head and said, "You two just can't not make with the movie quotes, can you?"

"What can I say," said Hope. "We need professional help."

Vince returned to the names as Hope picked up her cell phone and started texting. He looked at the name of Bill Pullman's character, Bridget's husband, in *The Last Seduction*. Clay was his name. And, Berg's boyfriend was Mike. He started to remove letters and move them around in his mind. Then it hit Vince like a Bogart punch.

"Holy jalapeños! I got it!" he said.

"Hey, I do the alliterative food lines," said Hope.

"You mean you figured out who the next victim is?" asked an excited Gina.

"No," said Vince. "I know who the murderer is."

He kneeled between them and showed them the paper with the names.

"Take the 'M' off of 'Mike,' put it separately after what you have left. Then take 'Clay,' and put the 'c' before the 'y.'"

Gina and Hope said at the same time, "Ike M. Lacy!"

Vince nodded.

"Holy hominy grits," said Hope.

Vince stood up and did his pacing thing.

"Before I call the police, let's try to remember some things that Ike, which obviously is not his real name, said in front of us."

With his sharp memory, it didn't take Vince long to recall pertinent facts about Ike.

"At that first movie class, when the A/C was on the fritz, he made covert references to *Body Heat*. He talked about not needing 'any more bodies in here,' and that it was like 'Florida in July.'"

"Right, and the 'bodies' could refer to dead persons, and *Body Heat* takes place in Florida," said Hope.

Vince remembered another line from Ike.

"He also said something about getting an 'ice bucket' to chill water bottles. The mentioning of an ice bucket could be a reference to the ice pick used as a weapon in *Basic Instinct*. Damn it, I should have picked up on these clues earlier."

Gina reached over and squeezed Vince's arm.

"These statements by Ike don't exactly shout out, 'Look at me!' Don't be too hard on yourself."

Vince wasn't convinced.

"When I spoke with Cassandra, we went over male abuser traits. I see now where Ike showed feelings of inadequacy when he said something like he wasn't an authority on any topic."

"He's right! I remember that," Hope said to Gina.

"He also couldn't accept Dustin Hoffman as a strong character in *Marathon Man*, because the actor didn't fit the typical macho version of the hero. If Jewel was here, now, she would probably say he was projecting his own feelings of inferiority onto the story."

"And he knew Pauline Josephs from before, and, like, put her down, calling her a 'man-eater,' and referred to her as a femme fatale," said Hope.

Vince nodded vigorously.

"Right. He practically named her as a victim! Jesus, I can be dense. His thin-skinned nature at the coffee shop was obvious because he didn't like it when I disagreed with him about Mrs. Mulwray's complex character in *Chinatown*. To Ike, she was just 'filthy.'"

"Or when I tried to show a bigger perspective about Susan Hayward's Barbara in *I Want to Live*. He wanted to just blame the women for their situations," said Hope.

Gina thought for a minute before speaking.

"At the coffee shop, he sympathized with Travis Bickle's character in *Taxi Driver*. He thought Bickle was doing the world a service, by cleaning the world up of depraved women."

"I think that Ike sees himself as picking up where Travis left off," said Vince.

That scary thought hung in the room for a moment until Hope spoke.

"Looks like it's Newman and Douglas time."

Chapter Forty-seven

Monday Evening

Douglas put out a BOLO on Ike M. Lacy after Vince contacted the lieutenant. Newman called Vince after he and other police officers went to Ike's place near the Ben Franklin Parkway. He said that the killer wasn't there, and he had cleaned out the apartment. Newman said they would be checking for fingerprints, DNA, and any other evidence that linked Ike to the murders.

Vince was once again at Reggio's Restaurant in Roxborough, trying to exorcise his demons associated with the eatery. He repeated his walk down the narrow side street where Jewel died, hoping to release her ghost now that the man who desecrated the road had been wiped from the face of the earth. He didn't say much during his dinner with Gina, who reached out often to squeeze his hand, and Vince was reminded that she was there tethered to him like an emotional lifeline.

As they sipped their lattes and shared a piece of Italian rum cake, Gina asked Vince about his wife's taste in movies.

"Did she dislike any particular genres or topics?"

Vince thought for a couple of seconds.

"She was pretty open to all types of films. She was not drawn to action stories unless there were interesting characters in them. That's why she was okay with *Die Hard* or even *Alien*. She could do without too much violence and gore. I think she especially liked movies with a good sense of humor, and was a sucker for a witty romantic comedy."

Gina popped another fork loaded with rum cake into her mouth followed by a sip of her coffee.

"Tell me a few of her favorites," she said.

Vince let out a couple of chuckles just thinking about the films.

"She loved *When Harry Met Sally*, and *Sleepless in Seattle*. Well so do I. I had a really big crush on Meg Ryan, so there was that, too. We both enjoyed good chick flicks."

"How very evolved of you," said Gina, as she pointed her fork at him before diving in for another piece of cake. "Did she have a favorite film?"

Vince didn't need any time to answer.

"She loved *Heaven Can Wait*. It was such a fun satire on the very wealthy. But, it also had this positive theme of how well America worked when it was like a team with all the players working together for a common goal."

"Yeah, but it was kinda sad. I mean, the main character dies, twice in fact, as Joe and then as that guy, Leo."

"True, but Joe's essence is reincarnated in the starting quarterback. Even though he has no recollection of his past life, the connection he has with Julie Christie's character lives on, and the love they share survives."

Vince could see in Gina's moist eyes that she knew he was no longer just talking about a movie. She wiped her eyes, and then cut short the sentimentality.

"Well having ultra-handsome Warren Beatty probably was the real reason it was her favorite."

Vince laughed.

"I'm sure his winning the Super Bowl in the good looks department helped beat the competition."

***

Gina was driving her Ford Focus back to Vince's house when his cell phone buzzed.

"Who is it?" asked Gina so quickly she almost didn't take a breath.

"Relax. It's a text from Hope," said Vince. After reading, he said, "She, Mark and Evan arrived at the Barnes and Noble on Chemical Road. She said she was surprised so many people turned out for James' mother's book launch for the latest volume of her poetry. 'We're not talking Stephen King here,' she says."

"She has won a number of literary awards, so that helps," said Gina in an uninvolved monotone, followed by a more animated, "I thought maybe you were getting a message from Newman."

"No, I guess we'll just have to wait to see what happens," he said. But, Vince knew that for both Gina and himself, patience just didn't seem like a virtue.

Gina pulled into Vince's driveway. The policeman sitting in his cruiser waved to them as they walked to the entrance. Once inside, Gina and Vince sat on the brown couch in the family room. Jellybean meowed when they entered, and wasted no time in jumping onto Vince's lap. She purred loudly as she repeatedly rubbed her face against the sides of Vince's jaw, as he scratched her soft, furry neck and head.

"She wants to make sure you know that you are her person," said Gina.

Vince kissed the cat on her head and looked into her eyes as she stared at him.

"Like I could forget. You are the best cat in the whole world, you know that?"

Jellybean resumed her rubbing. The interspecies connecting was interrupted by another buzz emanating from Vince's phone. Jellybean jumped off of Vince as he pulled out his cell, and she sought comfort in Gina's lap. Vince looked at the display, and sprang out of the sofa, cursing.

"Shit, shit, shit!"

Gina stood up, causing Jellybean to leap onto the floor. The cat hid under the rocker near the sliding doors leading to the outside patio. Vince knew she sensed that danger had invaded the security of her home.

"What? It's Ike, isn't it?" asked Gina.

Vince nodded.

"He's congratulating me for figuring out he's the killer. He must be monitoring police chatter or found out about the cops going to his apartment. He says that if I want the whole story, so I can write another book, that I have to guess from the clues who the next victim will be. Gina, he says that he has her. He says I have until midnight to guess who it is, or she will die like the character Clay in *The Last Seduction*."

"How did he die, again?" asked Gina in almost a whisper.

Vince sat down again on the sofa before answering.

"Bridget sprayed Mace down his throat, stopping his ability to breathe."

Gina sat down next to Vince and wrapped her left arm around him.

"How horrible," she said. She looked at her watch.

"Yes, I only have a couple of hours," said Vince. "He wants me to text him back when, and if, I figure out who he has abducted. Not that I have any idea where he is, but he said that if he sees any police close by, he will kill her."

Vince closed his eyes and squeezed his forehead with his right hand.

"I'm obviously missing something. I have to concentrate."

Gina slid down to the end of the couch.

"Take off your shoes," she said, "and lie down. Close your eyes, and rest your head in my lap."

Vince did as she told him. He stretched out on his back, and felt the softness of Gina's thighs as he lowered his head onto them. She began to massage his temples. He still felt agitated.

"What's wrong with me!" he said. "A person's life can end. Why haven't I been able to see clearly?"

Gina continued her soothing rubbing.

"Sh, sh," she said.

With his eyes closed, he could hear Gina's calming voice, and actually pictured the letters she uttered, "Sh, sh." They sounded like the word they were a part of, "Hush."

He bolted into a sitting position. He turned to Gina and gave her a quick, and he knew, startling kiss.

"Thank you! You said 'Sh.' The last two letters of 'Hush.' That's why Ike left the DVD of *Hush, Hush Sweet Charlotte*."

Gina's grinning excitement that Vince figured out the reason for the movie at the crime scene transformed into wide-eyed confusion.

"I don't understand. How does the title help you with the name of the next victim?"

"It's just like the 'pj' for Pauline Josephs," he said. Vince saw that she still wasn't there yet, as she shook her head. "Who is the sexually liberated woman that Newman is involved with?"

Recognition blossomed on Gina's face as she said, "S. H. Samantha Hoffman."

Vince nodded his head.

"Ike even said that Dustin Hoffman's character in *Marathon Man* should have been killed off, but I didn't make the last name connection. Another clue I didn't pick up on. I have to text Ike back."

After about twenty seconds, there was a ping on Vince's cell. He saw the notification of the new text, opened the message, and read it.

"Ike says that I should go to the classroom of the Main Line Movie Academy where we had our class. He says that I must come alone, or he will kill Samantha."

Gina grabbed his arm.

"You can't! It's too dangerous! Call Douglas or Newman."

Vince shook his head.

"No. He'll kill Samantha without hesitation if police show up. I might be able to stop him alone."

Gina went to her purse and pulled out the gun Samantha helped her learn how to use.

"Take this. Shoot Ike if you get the chance."

Vince reached for the weapon, then withdrew his hand.

"No, I don't know how to use that thing. I'd probably shoot off my foot. I still have the key to the Academy. I'll be right back."

Vince went to his bedroom, and after a few minutes returned to Gina.

"You have to promise to stay here."

Gina began to protest.

"If you don't hear from me in two hours, call Newman and tell him where I went. I'm going to tell the policeman outside that Ike texted me and said he was planning an attack at the book signing if I didn't figure out who the next victim would be. After he heads for the bookstore, I'll leave."

Gina held him in her arms, and would not let go. Vince had to gently break her embrace. There were tears in her eyes.

"Silly thing to say, but please be careful," she said. Vince smiled.

"How's this for another cliché. I'll do my best."

He kissed Gina and headed out.

Chapter Forty-eight

Monday Night

Vince parked his Civic in the darkness of the street. He walked to the door of the Academy. There were lights which illuminated the doorway and the sign next to it on the wall with the name of the institution. It was almost midnight, and, of course, the place was closed. He took out the key and opened the door. There was an alarm system and Vince punched in the code to disarm it. He knew the numbers because he asked for them in case he had to set up the videos for his class when the Academy was closed. Vince was sure Ike had gained those same codes the way he did when he broke into the homes of his victims.

He walked deliberately, swiveling his head around like a surveillance camera, checking for breaches in his security. The door to his classroom was open. The space was dark, but as Vince entered, a projection was displayed on the screen. It was Samantha Hoffman, bound and gagged in a chair, wearing a long, dark-haired wig. Vince realized that she was being made to look like Linda Fiorentino's Bridget from *The Last Seduction*. Vince heard Lacy whistling the song "Stand by Your Man," before he addressed Vince.

"The illusion on the screen many times mirrors our reality," said Lacy.

The image on the screen disappeared, the lights came on, and Lacy, holding a gun, walked from a corner of the room to the center of the teaching platform, where Samantha sat.

"Come on down, Vince. There's plenty of room. Take a front row seat. Sorry, no popcorn."

Vince descended the steps and sat in the first row directly across from Samantha.

"You've played well, Vince. But, now it's the endgame, and it's quite possible that none of us here will be alive when it's over. But, I still intend to be a winner."

Lacy stopped to reach for a backpack that was on a table next to the lectern on the platform. He pulled out a can of Mace, and placed it on the table. Vince stiffened, and he saw a look of terror in Samantha's eyes as she struggled to free herself from the plastic straps that secured her.

"You like stories, right Vince? I mean that is one of the main reasons we watch films, isn't it? How about I tell you one. Oh, you can come up with the elevator pitch later, if you get a chance to write the screenplay."

Lacy hopped up onto the table, and punched the air with the gun to point out what he thought needed stressing.

"You know, Vince, you said it yourself, in this classroom. The treachery of women is biblical. Eve, Delilah, etc. My mother fell right into the genetic line of those notorious women. My father was tough. He had to be to make a living doing construction work. So what if he drank a bit. He needed some relief from doing the hard labor, and getting laid off when jobs were scarce. He had to keep my mom in line, reel in any self-indulgent spending. He didn't do any permanent damage, mind you, just roughed her up a little. And, because of that, she refused to perform her wifely duties."

Lacy pulled a bottle of water out of his backpack and took a sip.

"The water is cold," said Lacy. "Could have used it on the first night of our class. Oh, by the way, it was me who messed with the thermostat. Had to have a reason to drop those *Body Heat* clues. Anyway, my mother satisfied her lust with the owner of the grocery store where she worked. He was married and had kids, and wasn't about to leave his family for a tramp. My dad found out about the affair and left, because of her."

Vince fidgeted, stuffed his hands into his cargo pants pockets, and spoke.

"How long do we have to listen to this melodrama?"

Lacy jumped off of the table and the platform, and stuck the gun in Vince's face.

"I had to endure your self-righteous bullshit about how badly women were treated in films. So, now you're going to hear me out!"

Lacy lowered the gun and hopped back onto the platform.

"Mom, the weak person that she was, used the excuse of a little injury at work to start taking pain-killers. She became addicted, lost her job, and couldn't support us. So, she decided to get rid of me, like a bag of trash. I was in the foster child system until I broke out. Better to be on my own than with good old mom."

Lacy started to walk back and forth while addressing Vince.

"I like those movies with John Wayne, and the James Bond stories. Those were the real heroes boys could look up to. In today's films men are weak and have to be saved by ass-kicking females. The whole world has reversed itself, and men are in retreat. You know, I admired your old pal, Stanford Patterson. He established a great film festival in the Philadelphia area. And, I bet he was misunderstood. We always blame men for infidelity, but there's a good chance that ice sculpture pretending to be human, Faye Patterson, drove her husband to look elsewhere for affection. It was his misfortune that he was snared by that female abomination, Cassandra Kimble."

Lacy stopped pacing and pointed the gun at Vince.

"And you, Vince. What a traitor to your sex. The bitch tries to off you, and now you are her champion. Why don't you just castrate yourself and be done with it?"

Vince presented an off-putting smile.

"I'm happy as I am. But, if going trans is what someone wants, I say be who you really are. I'm a big fan of Lana Wachowski."

Lacy chuckled.

"At least you are consistent in your perversion, Vince. And, I have no desire to hurt you, unless you provoke me. No, you are here to witness the culmination of my trinity of retribution against the femme fatales who got away with it. That way, you can write your next tale, again based on a true story, so we can correct this revisionist trend toward glorifying female aberrations."

Lacy moved close to Samantha and ripped the tape covering her mouth. She began to scream. He reached for the can of Mace.

"It will be a pleasure to shut you up once and for all."

Lacy put the gun down on the counter, grabbed the Mace in one hand and squeezed Samantha's nostrils shut with the other so that her mouth was forced to open. Before he could spray the toxic substance, Vince slipped one of his throwing knives out of his right pocket and threw it at Lacy. The killer must have caught a glimpse of its metallic reflection and moved to his right. The blade penetrated Lacy's left shoulder. The Mace fell to the floor as Lacy yelled out in pain. Before Vince could get the other knife he brought out of his left pocket and into his right hand, Lacy retrieved the gun and got off a shot that hit Vince in his right upper arm. Vince screamed as the bullet seared his flesh.

"It looks like someone else will have to write your screenplay, Vince," said Lacy as he raised the gun and pointed it at Vince. But, before he could fire his weapon, a gunshot rang out to the left of Vince, and Lacy recoiled from the shot that hit him in the chest. He dropped the gun and his soon-to-be lifeless body fell to the floor. Vince turned around and saw Gina still aiming the gun she had fired. She then lowered it and ran toward Vince, her cell phone already in her hand. She started to dial 911. After calling the emergency number she ripped part of Vince's shirt and tied it above Vince's wound. He and Samantha were stunned and speechless. Gina turned to Samantha.

"Thanks for the lessons," Gina said.

Chapter Forty-nine

Tuesday Afternoon

The white room looked blurry as Vince tried to focus on the shapes in front of him. He felt gentle pressure on his left hand. He swiveled his head, but it felt like a slow-motion pan until he stopped and realized it was Gina, smiling at him, now enveloping his fingers in a protective cocoon. His vision started to sharpen.

"Hey you," he said to her in a quiet voice.

"Drink some water," she said, as she pushed a cup with a straw near his mouth. As he sipped, the hospital room became more real to him and he understood why he was there. He pushed a button on the bed control remote and as his head raised up he saw that he had several visitors. James Player smiled at him and gave him a Schwarzenegger *Terminator:2* thumbs up.

"I knew you'd be bach," said James, in a bad Austrian accent.

Vernon had his arm around his son, Evan.

"Ah, Vince, you may be one, ah, of the few writers who lives out his stories before he writes them," said Vernon.

Newman and Samantha Hoffman were in the corner, holding onto each other like they would never be separated again. They didn't say anything. Vince now remembered he heard Samantha tell the police that Ike had drugged and abducted her just outside her house, as he had done with the other women. Her drooping tired eyes gazed at Vince, and he thought he saw gratitude in them.

"I'm guessing that the surgery was a success," asked Vince, as he turned back to Gina. "I gave you HIPPA clearance after my last rodeo, so what's the verdict?"

"It was a through-and-through wound, with no vascular, nerve, or bone damage. And, don't call me Clarence."

"Oh boy," said Vince with an anemic laugh, "she's rearranging quotes from the film *Airplane!* Definitely going up the movie geek ladder."

The room spun a bit, and Vince rubbed his eyes.

"Still feeling a bit woozy," he said.

"They had to clean out any infection and stitch your arm. They did dope you up some," said Gina.

Vince felt a soft punch to his right leg. It came from Hope who stood to his side with Mark behind her.

"Speaking of dope, what were you thinking, you idiot!" she said. "You're not perfect, but you're the only dad I have. Nobody warming up in the bullpen. Can't you let the police do their job for a change?"

Vince shrugged.

"Ike planned on killing Samantha no matter what. I honestly thought that if he even smelled a cop nearby, he would have thrown out his script and improvised a quick execution. I figured I could find a chance to take him down."

"Well, that's it," said Hope. "I'm taking away your knives. It's a good thing you had Gina there to save your ass."

Vince stroked Gina's hand.

"Lucky is what I am," he said.

At that moment Lt. Harvey Douglas marched into the room, with not a wrinkle in his jacket or a smile on his face. Right behind him was Jake, with his digital recorder in his hand.

"There's my brother, still acting like he's Woodward or Bernstein," said Vince.

"I write better than they do. I'm interviewing you next," said Jake. "By the way, how are you feeling?"

"See how the story comes first, and then my health," said Vince.

"My, my, my," said Douglas, not only looking like Tommy Lee Jones in *The Fugitive*, but sounding like him. "I told you right from the get-go that I didn't trust working with amateurs. This could have really gone south for you two, and I would have gotten the blame for it."

There was a momentary silence in the room. Then Douglas cracked a wide grin.

"So maybe you and Ms. Alimentare should join the PHPD. That way, I would be dealing with professionals in the future. She's a pretty good shot. We could use her."

Everyone broke out in relieved laughter.

"I think we'll stick to our civilian professions, Lieutenant," said Vince. He looked at Hope.

"So, did the doctor say I would be back to normal soon?" he asked.

"Normal?' said Hope with raised eyebrows. "Let's not push it. But, you should be able to play golf soon."

"Well if that's the case," said Vince, "I guess I'll have to take it up."

Epilogue

Six Months Later

Vince was relieved that this visit to Dr. Probst's office was for closure instead of being an opener. Since his PTSD symptoms were continually improving, he had not seen Probst for a couple of months. His psychologist was an okay guy, and he had GPS'ed Vince through some tricky emotional turns, but he was hoping the mental road ahead would be a bit easier to navigate.

"I'm pleased to hear that your nightmares have subsided, Vince," said Probst, as he cleaned his eyeglasses.

"I know your tell. The eyeglass thing means you think I'm conning you, but I'm not holding anything back. I am doing much better."

"Tell? This is a house of healing, Vince, not a house of games."

Vince laughed.

"My movie mania seems to be infecting the people around me. But, David Mamet would probably be pleased that a psychologist is referring to one of his films about a psychologist."

"As a person interested in the human mind, I am curious about what you have discovered about Ike M. Lacy that has helped you with your finding psychological resolution. The media has only provided superficial facts, without any analysis."

Vince eyed Probst sideways.

"I have a feeling your curiosity is about the size of a house full of cats. Anyway, his name is a phony. His real name is Abe Huserman. Once the police found out who he really is, they tracked down his background. His father, Martin, was not the positive role model his son says he was. He was arrested for drunk and disorderly episodes, mostly involving domestic incidents with his wife. He was verbally abusive toward her, according to police reports. He did push her around without beating her until he found out that she did have an affair, and then he did hit her. And, he was sexually demanding to the point that his wife called the police for being the victim of sexual violence. Ike, I mean Abe, presented him in our last encounter as just being a strong male."

"He was probably trying to live up to his father's expectations as to what a quote 'real man' is supposed to be. I would bet that his father belittled him while he was growing up."

Vince nodded.

"Newman read juvenile counseling records. Abe was not a big kid, shy, only average-looking with large ears, and his father kept riding him about what a weakling he was. Martin Huserman tried to push Abe into playing sports, and took him to football games. I mean he even played catch with the kid, so the boy probably interpreted that behavior as how his father was being a good dad. But, when Abe didn't excel, Martin would humiliate him."

Probst nodded his head, and there was a sad look on his face.

"I'm sure his father pushed him about proving his manliness with women. If the boy was shy, he probably wasn't successful, and that just incensed his angry father further. So, he saw women as sources of male failure. That's where his pathology toward females began."

Vince had more to add.

"Ike/Abe's interest in movies started with his father, who took him to see action films with macho males performing heroic deeds which attracted beautiful women characters. His father rented old John Wayne westerns, and James Bond films, and they watched them together. So, when his mother didn't succumb to her husband's brutish sexual behavior, Abe saw her as being a villain in the movie of his father's life. When Martin left and disappeared from his son's world, mom was to blame in Abe's mind."

Probst leaned forward in his chair.

"Can you tell me more about Abe's mother?"

"Again, there was more to the story than what Abe provided," said Vince. "Her name is Jodie. Since all she received was aggression from her husband, she did seek caring affection elsewhere. She was trying to hold down two jobs because her husband kept losing employment due to his drinking and anger. She had an affair with her employer. He was in a bad marriage, wanted to leave, but his wife became ill. He had children to care for, and felt he couldn't leave his family. Jodie hurt her back on the job, and became addicted to opioids, like so many other Americans. After her husband split, there was no one to take care of her son. She lost her job and her health care. She put Abe up for adoption because she felt she was too damaged to take care of him. She tried to reconcile with him many times once she was clean and sober, but he refused."

"What a sad story," said Probst.

"Yes, for him, and the victims of violence against women everywhere," said a grim Vince.

After a pause, Vince smiled and spoke again.

"But, I do have some good news."

"Let's hear it. I don't get the good stuff in this job often enough. People usually stop keeping in touch after they get back on track."

"I'll send you a movie gift card at Christmas so you won't feel neglected," said Vince. "Anyway, Jake is getting a great deal of attention about his inside story on his brother's latest confrontation with a killer. There's talk of a Pulitzer. He's always riding my coattails."

"Remember when I told you a while back that you don't have to worry about becoming as famous as Lady Gaga? I may have been wrong about that."

"Guess I'll have to get fitted for an outfit made out of meat," said Vince.

"So with what's been happening with Jake, I guess that must mean another book is on the way, right?" said Probst.

Vince nodded his head.

"This time, Vernon and his son, Evan, will be the co-authors with Jake. I'm spreading around the workload. And, we already have a deal for a movie. James Player and I will do the screenplay. That should score some major points with James' successful parents. I just hope he will cut down on his movie tangents while we are working together, and not be a pain in the ass."

"Well, knowing you, the ass pain can go both ways," said Probst.

"Hey, I'm the patient here, so be supportive," said Vince with mock outrage. He then added, "But, there's more."

"This is sounding like one of those cable ads where you get an extra set of steak knives if you buy the miracle kale shredder."

"Please don't mention kale when I'm trying to be positive," said Vince. "There's more to celebrate. I helped Cassandra sell her screenplay about her dystopian unsocials. The proceeds from her deal and mine will be donated to organizations that work to end violence against women."

"That's great to hear," said Probst as he eyed up Vince, who knew his face still looked like he had more to offer.

"Okay, what else?" he asked.

"You're such a therapist, being all perceptive and all," said Vince. "Why don't you guess"

Probst rubbed his chin.

"I already know that Hope found an apartment, and Mark Goodner has moved in with her. Nothing to add to that story?"

"No, except that she and Mark are good together. And, their place being only fifteen minutes away makes me feel like I'll still be a supporting player in her life."

"Anything else going on with Newman and Samantha Hoffman since they have been sharing the same space?" asked Probst.

"Newman says he was okay with giving up his apartment and likes living in Samantha's townhouse. He negotiated having one of the bedrooms set up to watch sports and house all of his Eagles and Phillies memorabilia. You have to know a secret knock to get in, which I don't think he has shared with Samantha. Anyway, do you give up on the last bit of good tidings?"

Probst's face morphed from one of constricted concentration to one of relaxed enlightenment.

"It has to do with you and Gina," said Probst. You're engaged!"

"Bingo, Doc! You win that set of steak knives."

"Are you kidding with all of this? It sounds like you are writing a happy ending to a movie to make everyone feel good as the story ends."

"Once in a while, it's encouraging to know that things can work out for the best," said Vince.

"Well, you have come a long way from that pessimistic patient that first sat in that chair. Will I be invited to the wedding?"

"Of course, Doc," said Vince. "As long as you don't tack on the nuptials as part of your therapy bill."

Probst laughed.

"I won't if you don't pull a male version of the Julia Roberts role, and become a runaway groom."

"You're joking, but I wouldn't be surprised if someone is writing that script right now," said Vince.

"Do you know where you will be going on your honeymoon?" asked Probst.

"Where else?" said Vince. "Hollywood."

About the Author

Augustus Cileone won the Dark Oak Mystery Contest sponsored by Oak Tree Press, for the novel, *A Lesson in Murder*, about homicides associated with a Philadelphia Quaker school. His second novel, *Feast or Famine*, a satire, deals with a traumatized man dealing with his Catholic Italian American upbringing in the 1960's and 1970's. He has been honored for his writing by *Annual Art Affair*, *Hidden River Arts*, the annual *Writer's Digest* writing competition for two plays, *The Philadelphia Writers' Conference*, the *Montgomery County Community College's Annual Writers' Club Poetry and Fiction Contest*, *Filmmakers International Screenwriting Awards*, and the *Annual StoryPros International Screenplay Contest*. His short stories appear in the anthologies entitled *South Philly Fiction* and *Death Knell V*, and in the literary periodical Schuylkill Valley Journal.

This novel is the follow-up to, "Out of the Picture."

Augustus also has a movie blog available at the following address:

http://mymeaningfulmovies.blogspot.com